Dare to collect them all!

Dare to collect them all!

More books from The Midnight Library:
Nick Shadow's terrifying collection continues . . .

THE MIDNIGHT LIBRARY

Blind Witness

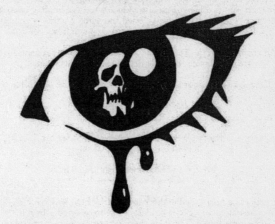

Nick Shadow

Hodder Children's Books

A division of Hachette Children's Books

The Midnight Library: Volume XII

Stories by Shaun Hutson

CONTENTS

Dare to collect them all!

More books from The Midnight Library:
Nick Shadow's terrifying collection continues . . .

THE MIDNIGHT LIBRARY

Blind Witness

Nick Shadow

Hodder
Children's
Books

A division of Hachette Children's Books

The Midnight Library: Volume XII

Stories by Shaun Hutson

CONTENTS

Dare to collect them all!

More books from The Midnight Library:
Nick Shadow's terrifying collection continues . . .

THE MIDNIGHT LIBRARY

Blind Witness

Nick Shadow

*Hodder
Children's
Books*

A division of Hachette Children's Books

Special thanks to Shaun Hutson

Copyright © 2007 Working Partners Limited
Illustrations copyright © 2007 David McDougall
Created by Working Partners Limited, London W6 0QT

First published in Great Britain in 2007
by Hodder Children's Books

1

A Catalogue record for this book is available from the British Library

ISBN-10: 0 340 93026 8
ISBN-13: 978 0 340 93026 7

Typeset in Weiss Antiqua by Avon DataSet Ltd,
Bidford-on-Avon, Warwickshire

Printed and bound in Great Britain by
Clays Ltd, St Ives plc

The paper and board used in this paperback by Hodder Children's Books
are natural recyclable products made from wood grown in
sustainable forests. The manufacturing processes conform to the
environmental regulations of the country of origin.

Hodder Children's Books
a division of Hachette Children's Books
338 Euston Road, London NW1 3BH
An Hachette Livre UK company

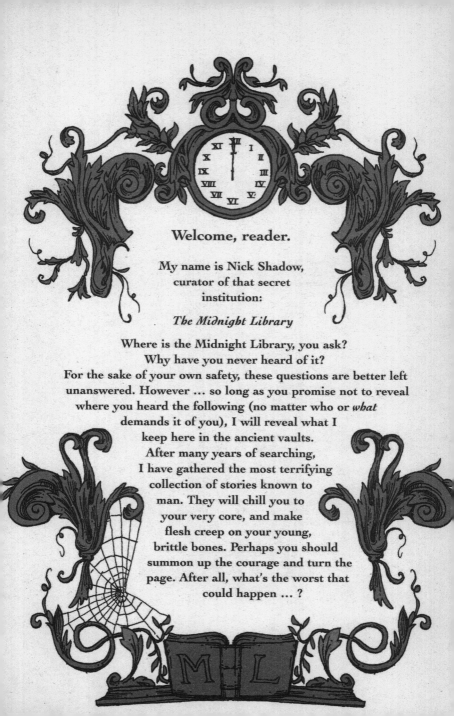

Welcome, reader.

My name is Nick Shadow,
curator of that secret
institution:

The Midnight Library

Where is the Midnight Library, you ask?
Why have you never heard of it?
For the sake of your own safety, these questions are better left
unanswered. However ... so long as you promise not to reveal
where you heard the following (no matter who or *what*
demands it of you), I will reveal what I
keep here in the ancient vaults.
After many years of searching,
I have gathered the most terrifying
collection of stories known to
man. They will chill you to
your very core, and make
flesh creep on your young,
brittle bones. Perhaps you should
summon up the courage and turn the
page. After all, what's the worst that
could happen ... ?

The Midnight Library: Volume XII

Stories by Shaun Hutson

CONTENTS

BLIND
WITNESS

Breakfast time wasn't the same without his mum around.

Liam Webb sat at the kitchen table eating cereal.

He looked at the clock on the wall opposite and noticed that it was almost eight a.m.

Normally his mum would have been chattering away, telling him to hurry up with his breakfast. Reminding him about his homework while she prepared his lunch. Every now and then she'd turn the radio up and sing along when one of her favourite songs came on. That had always made Liam smile, no matter what kind of mood he'd been in that morning.

But not this morning. Not since she'd left a month earlier.

He felt as if his whole life had changed since she'd been gone and, at times, he missed her so badly it was like a physical pain.

He heard footfalls on the stairs.

'Morning, Liam.'

His dad's voice echoed around the kitchen as he walked in and headed for the kettle on the worktop. He was a big man. Over six feet tall and powerfully built. Tattoos ran down both his forearms and his hair was cut very short. You wouldn't want to pick a fight with Liam's dad.

'Hi, Dad,' Liam murmured. He didn't look up.

'Sleep all right?' his dad asked.

'Yes, thanks,' Liam said, keeping his head down. He finished his breakfast and carried the bowl over to the dishwasher.

'In a hurry?' his dad asked, as he put two slices of bread into the toaster. He leaned across the counter and forced Liam to make eye contact with him. Liam glanced at his dad and looked quickly away. The atmosphere was as difficult as it had always been since his mum had gone. She'd left them alone together, and they didn't even know how to have a conversation.

'I've got to get ready for school,' Liam said, desperate to get away.

'You've another forty minutes before you've got to be there. What's your rush?' his dad asked. 'When I was your age I never wanted to get to school.'

'There are things I have to do,' Liam stammered, walking quickly towards the kitchen door.

'Like what?' snapped his dad, pouring himself some coffee.

'Dad, I just need to get ready, that's all,' Liam insisted. 'I've got to get to school early to finish off a project.'

His dad shook his head dismissively and continued sipping his coffee.

'You always seem keen to get out when I'm around,' he said, his voice low and quiet. Almost like a growl.

Liam didn't answer.

Tell him the truth, Liam thought to himself. *Tell him you can't stand to be around him*. But he knew he couldn't. He was too terrified of how his dad would react. Now that Liam's mum wasn't around any more to calm him down . . .

'I know you blame me for your mum leaving,' his dad said suddenly. Liam paused in the doorway. Had he just heard right? Was his dad actually admitting that this was all his fault? Liam turned slowly round.

'I didn't say that,' Liam said carefully.

'You don't have to!' his dad exclaimed, slamming his coffee mug down on the kitchen table. Liam couldn't help jumping.

'I'm going to school,' Liam said, turning back round. 'See you later.'

His dad didn't answer.

Liam hurried into the hall, grabbed his schoolbag

and walked out of the front door. He pulled it shut behind him and paused for a moment, leaning back against the door. He let out a long sigh of relief, then set off down the street.

Unlike nearly everyone else he knew at school, Liam actually looked forward to classes. They got him out of the house.

He paused as he reached the top of the hill that led down to St Luke's school. Then he began to run, his heart leaping with exhilaration as he hurtled down the steep slope.

'Don't worry, they won't start school without you.' The shout startled Liam and he glanced sharply behind him.

Across the road he saw two boys making their way down the hill.

His heart sank.

Wesley Brown and Joshua Clemence.

The *terrible two*, Liam called them. Wesley had carrot-red hair and a temper. Joshua was a typical sidekick – too scared to stand up to Wesley, despite his stocky physique.

'Do you always run to school, Liam?' Wesley asked, as they sauntered across the road to join him.

'You should do cross country as well as all those other after-school clubs you do,' Josh added. 'Then you could get there even faster.'

The two boys laughed.

'Your mum used to drive you to school, didn't she?' Wesley said, still grinning. 'Is that why you have to walk now? Because she left you?'

'That's none of your business,' Liam said. He felt his face go red as he struggled not to get upset. He couldn't stand someone like Wesley talking about his mum.

'Ooooh, sorry,' Wesley sneered. 'You're not going to start crying, are you?'

'It'd take more than you to make me cry,' Liam snapped. He tried to pick up pace as he walked down the hill, hoping to lose the two boys. But it was no good. They weren't going to let him get away.

'You'd cry if they shut down the school, wouldn't you?' Josh asked. 'You'd have nowhere else to go. I mean, you haven't got any friends, have you?'

'Leave him, Josh,' Wesley grinned. 'He's too busy trying to concentrate on what he's going to do in school today.' Wesley tapped Liam on the back of the head. 'Aren't you, Liam?'

Liam could feel the anger building up inside him. He looked at the other two boys and wished that the school ran a class in karate. He'd learn how to flatten them both. They reached the bottom of the hill. The school gates were in sight, thank goodness.

'Science club today, isn't it?' Wesley asked. 'That's where you're going after school, right?'

Liam nodded.

'What are you studying?' Josh asked.

'The acidity of rain in the area,' Liam said, knowing how square he sounded.

'Wow,' Josh said, faking excitement. 'That sounds really interesting.' He paused. 'Not.'

Josh and Wesley both laughed loudly.

Liam walked on, trying to ignore his two companions.

'If you looked up nerd on the internet,' Wesley chuckled, 'there'd be a picture of Liam.'

'Yeah, you spend more time at school than you do at home,' Josh chimed in. 'That's not normal.'

'*Liam's* not normal,' Wesley continued.

'I like school,' Liam snapped. 'I like learning new things.'

'Ooohhh, stressy,' the other two boys said in unison, laughing at their perfectly co-ordinated response.

Liam was just grateful that they didn't know the real reason he preferred school to home.

'See you around, nerd,' Wesley said as they approached the school playground. He gave Liam a farewell punch in the arm and sauntered off, Josh following. Liam watched them leave, rubbing his arm. Thank God they'd gone.

The school was a collection of new, white-painted buildings gathered around the original red-brick school building. Liam wandered across the playground, past pupils standing in twos chatting or messing about in larger groups. Every now and then, someone would glance at him and nod a hello. But no one came over to speak to Liam. He headed towards the main doors of the school and pulled out his homework as he waited for the bell to ring.

Since Liam's mum had left, even the people he'd previously been friendly with seemed to find it hard to speak to him. Perhaps they were worried about upsetting him if they mentioned her. Plus, he had to admit that he'd become a bit of a loner since she'd left. Turned in on himself. He simply didn't feel like talking to people like he had done before.

The bell sounded loudly and Liam pushed his homework back into his bag as he got to his feet. Two teachers pushed the main doors open. They stood at the doorway like a couple of security guards as students piled past them into the school hallway. Liam joined the people pushing through the doors. Another school day had begun.

* * *

'Right, go on, clear off, you lot.'

Mr Parker waved his arms in the direction of the science lab door.

'And don't run,' the teacher reminded them, trying to shout above the noise of raised voices and the clanging of the school bell.

Liam sat at his desk near the back of the class, not moving.

He watched as the class emptied. The shouts and catcalls gradually died away as the rest of the class made their way down the corridor.

Mr Parker turned to Liam.

'Science club's cancelled today, Liam,' he said, walking towards Liam's desk. 'I told you that.'

'I know, Mr Parker, but I was wondering if it'd be all right for me to stay and carry on with my project anyway.' Liam hoped his teacher would say yes. He *really* didn't want to go home yet. His dad would only want to have another conversation like the one this morning.

Mr Parker sucked in a deep breath.

'Well, you can if you want to,' he said. 'But I won't be able to help you much. I've a lot of test papers to mark.'

'I'll be quiet as a mouse,' Liam assured his teacher. *Thank goodness!*, he thought.

Mr Parker smiled. 'Anybody would think you didn't want to go home.'

Liam forced a smile.

If only you knew.

'So I can stay?' Liam checked.

'You won't have the lab to yourself. I'll be here, marking papers,' Mr Parker said. 'Don't forget to put goggles and gloves on before you touch the acid bottles.'

Liam shook his head and smiled, getting to his feet as Mr Parker sat down at his desk.

Liam's teacher dug a hand into his trouser pocket and pulled out a small silver key that he handed over to Liam.

'The key to the acid cupboard,' Mr Parker said, before pulling an exercise book off the pile.

The padlocked cupboard that housed the bottles

of acid sat on the wall at the far end of the laboratory. Far enough away so that Liam wouldn't disturb his teacher. Liam picked up the silver key. Then he went to the large cardboard box that was filled to the brim with plastic goggles and protective latex gloves.

Liam found a pair of gloves and pulled them on, testing them for size. He began trying on the goggles, searching for a pair that would fit him.

Bang! The thud on the classroom window made him spin round.

Two of Liam's fellow pupils were pulling faces at him through the wide windows of the science lab.

'Creep!' one of them shouted. Then they both ran off laughing.

Liam shook his head and looked over at his teacher. But Mr Parker was bent over his desk. He couldn't have heard a thing. Liam turned back to looking through the box of goggles.

The first ones were too small, the next two pairs too large and, when he finally found some that were a good fit, he was dismayed to see that the strap used to fasten them around his head was broken.

'Why don't people take more care of things?' Liam muttered irritably to himself. 'Just because they don't belong to them.'

Liam selected one of the larger pairs. They didn't fit as tightly as they should have done but it was better than nothing.

He put the goggles on to the nearest workbench and walked over to the acid cupboard. He unlocked the padlock and pulled open the doors.

Inside were tidy rows of glass bottles with glass stoppers and red labels with skull and crossbones. Hydrochloric acid. Sulphuric acid. Nitric acid. The bottles looked so neat and harmless, it was difficult to imagine that the clear liquids were deadly.

Liam grabbed a bottle of hydrochloric acid and placed it on the bench, next to a row of test tubes in a wooden holder.

'Everything all right over there?' Mr Parker called.

'Yes thanks, sir,' Liam replied.

Outside, the first spots of rain began to spatter the large windows that looked out over the school playing-field.

'Great,' Liam muttered to himself.

He pulled on his goggles, swearing quietly when they slipped down his nose. He couldn't even get a pair of goggles to fit him right! He reached for the bottle of hydrochloric acid and carried it carefully back to the workbench. Then he went back to the cupboard and pulled out a bottle of sulphuric acid and another of concentrated nitric acid.

The glass stopper in the bottle of nitric acid rattled as he set it down angrily on the workbench. He couldn't shake off his bad mood. Still, at least he'd been allowed to stay behind after school. That had to count for something, even if he did have to put up with idiots banging on the classroom window.

He took out the stopper from the bottle of nitric acid. A tiny drop of acid dripped from the stopper.

It hung in the air for a second, like a lethal tear. Then it fell to the floor.

Everything seemed to move in slow motion as Liam realized what was happening. He watched as the drop of acid hit the rubber matting around the workbench.

It ate through the rubber easily and burned a small hole in the floor. A tiny plume of smoke rose up.

Liam jumped back, alarmed at the damage the acid had done.

'Wow!' he exclaimed.

'Are you all right, Liam?' Mr Parker asked, looking up.

'Yes thanks,' Liam told the teacher, hastily putting his foot over the damage to the floor.

Mr Parker raised a thumb in salute and bent back to his work.

Liam put the stopper back in the bottle.

Powerful stuff, he thought. He carefully set the concentrated nitric acid down next to the other bottles. He readjusted the goggles on his nose, and sighed as they automatically slipped back down. He tried to fasten them more tightly but it was no good.

'Hey, nerd.'

Liam turned towards the window.

'Oh, no,' he murmured as he saw Wesley Brown and Joshua Clemence standing outside, gazing in at him as if he was a goldfish in a bowl.

'You look like a mad scientist,' Josh called, bouncing a football on the tarmac.

Liam waved them away, wanting to get back to his project.

'No, you look more like an alien,' Wesley said, laughing loudly. 'A nerd from outer space.' Both of them were shouting to make themselves heard through the glass of the science lab window.

They laughed.

Liam shook his head and turned his back on them, determined to get on with his work. He knew they'd get fed up standing there and just go away.

Wouldn't they?

'See you, nerd,' Wesley shouted.

'Geek,' Josh added, and both boys dashed off on to the playing-field, kicking the ball ahead of them.

Liam watched them for a moment, then shook his head and filled a beaker with water from the tap in front of him. He did the same with some hydrochloric acid, tipping it carefully into a test tube that was propped in the holder he'd taken from the cupboard. Liam reached for a piece of litmus paper that was lying on the worktop nearby and inserted it into the water, watching the paper change colour.

He made a note of the colour and the acidity level, then selected a fresh piece of litmus paper and did the same with the hydrochloric acid.

His goggles slipped down his nose slightly and he pushed them back with one finger.

Liam turned and looked out of the window at the field.

Wesley and Josh were still kicking their ball around, seemingly oblivious to the rain that was still falling.

Losers, Liam thought.

He turned back to his experiment and reached for the bottle of concentrated nitric acid, annoyed that they had broken his concentration. But he couldn't help glancing out of the window again.

They were playing keepie-uppie with the football while they waved stupidly at him.

Liam gritted his teeth, unscrewed the stopper and set it down. The strong acid smell filled his nostrils. It reminded him of the stuff his mum used to unblock drains.

He carefully began pouring the lethal liquid into the test tube, only too aware that this acid could eat through his latex glove in seconds. He watched as the clear liquid ran into the test tube. Holding his breath, he tried to keep his hands steady.

Careful.

BANG!

A loud thud made the glass of the window vibrate.

Liam jumped violently. His safety goggles slid from his nose and hit the worktop with a dull crack.

Startled, he dropped the bottle of nitric acid and the test tube.

The test tube shattered. Glass and acid flew into the air.

It all happened so fast. Liam didn't have a chance to do a thing. Angry drops of acid flew into his face, burning his eyeballs. Liam heard an agonized scream echo around the classroom. Then he realized that the screams came from him.

He felt as if someone had stuck red-hot needles into his eyes.

'Help!' he shrieked, rubbing at his eyes, trying to wipe away both the acid and the unbearable pain.

He blindly scrambled for the tap close to him, but it was no good – he had completely lost his bearings. The pain forced him to his knees and he banged his head against the cool rubber tiles of the floor. Anything to take the edge off the searing hot needles that stabbed his eyes.

White light burned behind his eyelids, then slowly faded to suffocating darkness. Liam was half aware of the shouts of his teacher and someone rolling him over, trying to pull his hands away. Liam screamed again as he felt himself being pinned down. The pain filled his whole head – *please, someone stop this!* With a final gasp, Liam let his body go limp in his teacher's arms. He gave himself up to the pain.

Liam woke in darkness.

He tried to open his eyes, but something was pressing down on his eyelids. Fingers shaking, he lifted a hand and gingerly felt his face. Wads of cotton were taped over his eyes.

'No!' Liam said under his breath. Now he could remember. Remembered the slam of the football, the slip of the hand, the searing pain, then . . . nothing.

'Where am I?' he said out loud. No one answered.

Questions tumbled through his mind and he closed his hand over a sheet that lay across him. He realized that he was moving; he could feel the rhythmic rattle of wheels beneath him. He was being pushed along.

'Liam?'

He recognized the voice immediately.

Dad.

'Liam, can you hear me?' his dad asked.

Liam nodded slowly.

'You're in hospital,' his dad told him. 'You're on your way to surgery.'

'My eyes,' Liam began, lifting a hand to feel his face.

'I know,' his dad interrupted. 'I know what happened. I know about the acid. Your teacher told me. I'm here for you, Liam,' his dad said, his voice cracking. 'I came to the hospital as soon as I could.'

Liam felt the muscles of his body tighten. Since when did his dad do affection? Liam knew he should have been grateful, but he only felt embarrassed. He'd never heard his dad get emotional before – not like this.

'There'll be minimal scarring to your face,' said his dad, trying to reassure him.

I hadn't even thought about scarring! Liam thought. *Great. Now I have even more to worry about.*

'Most of the acid went in your eyes.'

A new thought hit Liam.

'I'm going to be blind, aren't I?' Liam asked, as he felt the trolley turn a corner.

'The acid *has* damaged both eyes,' his dad said,

21

sounding uncomfortable. 'But you're going to be all right. You've been lucky. The doctor said they can do a cornea transplant. They can give you your sight back. That's great, isn't it?'

Liam nodded, though he wasn't sure. What was so great? The fact that he'd have to have an operation on his eyes?

He felt like crying.

Liam raised a hand to touch his bandaged face again and turned his head in the direction of another set of footsteps he heard walking next to the trolley.

'Hello, Dr Newman,' Liam heard his dad say. Funny how respectful he sounded. Liam didn't often hear his dad talk in such a reverential way.

A strong hand closed around one of Liam's. It felt so reassuring. Much more reassuring than anything his dad had to say.

'How are you feeling, young man?' asked the doctor.

Do you want the honest answer? Liam thought to himself. But he knew he had to pretend to be strong and brave.

'OK, I suppose,' Liam answered. So much for being strong and brave!

'Well, you've nothing to be afraid of now,' Dr Newman told him. 'You're in safe hands.' It was as if the doctor knew exactly how Liam was feeling.

'What are you going to do to my eyes?' Liam asked.

'Well,' the doctor said. 'You'll be delighted to know that we have a donor. That means we'll be able to remove the corneas from his eyes and give them to you. I can explain the procedure to you if you like.'

'No, thanks,' Liam said. He felt bad enough. He could do without the gory details.

'Oh, all right then,' Dr Newman laughed. 'All you really need to know is that it's a routine operation. You won't even have to go under general anaesthetic. And the best news of all is that you'll be able to go home a few hours after the operation is completed. You'll be able to go home with your dad. That's good news, isn't it?'

'Terrific,' Liam mumbled.

'That's great, son,' Liam heard his dad say

23

awkwardly. Liam wondered if Dr Newman had any idea how much he and his dad hated being together.

'We can do the operation right now,' Dr Newman told Liam. 'You'll be home by tomorrow teatime.'

Liam suddenly realized there was something he *did* want to know.

'Who's the donor?' Liam asked.

'We can't tell you that I'm afraid, Liam,' the doctor said. 'Hospital policy. People who receive organs from donors aren't allowed to know who they've come from.'

Liam nodded. He guessed he could understand that.

'What if the operation isn't a success?' he asked quietly.

'There's no reason why it shouldn't be,' Dr Newman told him. 'I've performed the operation myself several times and it's always been successful. There's nothing for you to worry about. As I said, by this time tomorrow you'll be home with your dad again.' The doctor patted Liam's knee reassuringly. All around them were the noises of the hospital – bleepers going off, telephones ringing. And the smell! That strong, overwhelming smell of bleach. Liam knew the doctor was trying to be kind, but it was difficult to feel reassured.

'I'll take a couple of days off work,' his dad said, interrupting Liam's thoughts. 'Just until you get used to the . . . to your . . .'

'To my new eyes?' Liam finished the sentence for him. His dad was so uptight! He couldn't even put Liam's accident into words.

'Until you're feeling better,' his dad said quickly. 'I'm sure they can manage at work without me for two days.'

'I'll be all right on my own,' Liam said. *I have been so far*, he thought. *Why should this accident make a difference?*

'I said I'll take time off and I will,' his dad snapped. 'I don't want you falling over things because you can't see properly.' He leaned closer to Liam. 'I'll tell you something else. I reckon those two boys who caused this should be dealt with, don't you?'

Liam sighed. Plots for revenge. Like he needed them.

The operation and then two days at home, stuck in the house with his dad. He wasn't sure which he was dreading the most.

'The operation went well, the doctor said.'

Liam was sitting next to his dad in the car and could feel the engine rev as his dad pulled away from the hospital. Even if it meant being back with his dad, Liam was flooded with relief – the operation *had* been a success. Just like Dr Newman had said it would be.

'Thank goodness,' Liam nodded. He lifted one hand to his face and felt the thick plastic eye shields that protected both of his eyes. They were held in place by a single strip of bandage.

'I'll be around to help until you can manage on your own,' his dad reminded him. 'I've taken two days off work for you, Liam. You should be grateful for that.'

'I didn't ask you to,' Liam said quietly.

'What did you think I was going to do?' his dad asked. 'Let you stumble around bumping into things? I just want you to realize the sacrifices I'm making to be with you. Work could really do with me at the moment.'

'Thanks,' Liam said as he felt the car pull to a halt.

'You don't have to thank me, Liam,' his dad said, switching off the engine. What was this man on? He'd just given Liam a lecture about how grateful he should be!

I can't do right for doing wrong, Liam thought to himself, frustration simmering. But it was no good. No good pointing this out to his dad. He wouldn't listen. He could hear his dad walking around to the passenger-side door and yanking it open for Liam to get out.

Liam felt his dad's arm around him, pulling him from the car. The two of them made their way to the front door, Liam reluctantly holding his dad's arm so that he wouldn't trip over.

He heard the key scrape in the lock and the front door swing open. His dad guided him carefully into the hall, closing the door behind them.

'The only thing you need to think about for the next

few days is getting plenty of rest, like the doctor said,' Liam's dad reminded him. 'Then you can go back to school. Forget the accident ever happened. By the way, while you were in hospital, there were some get well cards for you. Two boys from your class delivered them.'

'I'll have a look when I can see them,' Liam said. He was surprised – and glad – that someone had taken the time to think about him.

Liam let his dad lead him up to his bedroom, stumbling a couple of times on the stairs.

'If I was you, I'd go straight to sleep,' his dad advised. 'It's late.'

'What time is it?' Liam asked.

'Almost eleven o'clock,' his dad informed him. 'You get a good night's sleep. If you want anything, just call me.'

Liam nodded. He sat down gratefully on the edge of his bed and felt the mattress sink below him. He already felt tired.

'I've just a few phone calls to make,' his dad added.

'At this time of night?' Liam asked, leaning back on the pillows.

'They're to do with work,' his dad said. 'Nothing for you to worry about. Just go to bed.'

'Goodnight,' Liam said.

He heard his bedroom door close as his dad stepped out on to the landing, then Liam heard the footfalls on the stairs.

Liam suddenly felt very alone in his bedroom. The fact that he couldn't see anything – couldn't see any of his familiar belongings – didn't help. He didn't even know if the light was on or off.

Feeling his way around the room, Liam found the chest of drawers that stood close to his bed. He fumbled for the handle on the top drawer and pulled, searching inside for a pair of pyjamas. He pulled some pieces of clothing out, not sure what colour they were or even whether or not he had a jacket and trousers.

For a moment he wondered about calling to his dad for help but then decided against it.

He managed to remove his clothes and climb into

the pyjamas without too much trouble. It was a short walk across the landing to the bathroom. He'd clean his teeth, he told himself, then get into bed. He stepped out of his room, keeping his back to the wall to guide himself, being careful not to knock anything over. Again he wondered if it might be more sensible to call his dad but, once more, he decided he'd rather manage by himself.

Liam was halfway across the landing when he heard a loud banging on the front door.

Who's calling at this time of night? Liam wondered.

He stood still, pressed against the wall, knowing that he was out of sight from the stairwell. Anyone looking up wouldn't be able to see him. For some reason, this mattered. Liam's nerves were on edge and he was suspicious, though he didn't know why.

There was another loud bang on the door.

Liam heard his dad moving swiftly across the hall below. He was muttering something under his breath as he opened the front door.

'What the hell are you doing here?' he heard his dad

ask. 'I've told you before. If you want to talk to me you do it at the club. Not at my house.'

Liam swallowed hard and willed himself to breathe as quietly as he could.

'It's important!' hissed the second voice. 'It couldn't wait.'

Liam felt a chill run down his spine. The second voice was low and gruff. Little more than a growl. He wondered what kind of man it belonged to.

'I told you we'd speak tomorrow,' his dad snapped.

'Well, our little problem won't wait until tomorrow,' the gruff voice insisted. 'That's why I'm here now.'

'Come in,' his dad rasped. 'I don't want people seeing you here. Besides, you make the place look untidy.'

Liam heard the front door slam behind the visitor.

'Now, what do you want?' his dad demanded. 'And make it quick. My son's upstairs.'

Liam gasped slightly. Why would his dad mention him? What did he have to do with anything? He could hear that the two men were still in the hallway.

'Like I said, I wouldn't have come here but things are

getting out of hand. That problem's got to be taken care of now. The man's getting cocky – too cocky,' Liam heard the man say.

'Then sort it,' his dad snapped. 'Do I have to deal with everything myself? Use your initiative. You know what's got to be done, so do it.'

'Like before?' the other voice wanted to know.

'Just like before,' Liam's dad answered. 'Take some help if you need it but take care of it. I want it sorted by this time tomorrow. And no mistakes.'

'Yeah, all right,' the second man said. 'And I'm sorry I came to your house but . . .'

'You will be sorry if you don't get out of here now,' hissed Liam's dad. 'You'll lose more than your job.'

Liam could hear the anger in his dad's voice. He wondered what he meant.

There was a moment's silence and then Liam heard the front door being opened.

'This time tomorrow night?' the gruff-voiced man asked.

'You heard!' Liam's dad snapped. 'Now go.'

Liam heard the front door close, and the sound of his dad's footsteps retreating back across the hall. For what seemed like for ever, Liam remained pressed up against the wall on the landing. He couldn't believe it. Whoever that man was, no matter how frightening his voice had sounded, he'd still been willing to take orders from Liam's dad.

Liam swallowed hard. His hands had bunched up into fists, his fingernails cutting into the flesh of his palms. Slowly, he forced his hands to relax and concentrated on slowing down his breathing. Liam realized he wasn't the only person to find his dad intimidating. No, not intimidating. *Terrifying*. The way his dad had spoken to that man . . . that wasn't the way anyone spoke to their colleagues! What was going on?

Liam crept back to his bedroom without cleaning his teeth. He just wanted to be alone in his room.

It was like looking through dirty windows.

His vision was blurry. The bed, the curtains, his

books and the TV set in the corner of his room seemed to be surrounded by a heat haze, their edges shimmering. But as Liam looked at his own smudged reflection in his bedroom mirror, he was grateful that he could see anything at all.

'Put the dark glasses on,' his dad said.

Liam reached for them and placed them on his nose. The darkness seemed to help and the blurred edges of some objects swam into focus as he turned to look at his dad. He could see the familiar old scar on his dad's neck as clearly as ever.

'How do your eyes feel?' his dad asked.

'OK. Don't worry,' Liam said. 'I'm going back to school today. You won't have to take any more time off work. I was getting sick of being stuck in the house anyway.'

His dad nodded.

'Do you want me to drop you off?' he asked.

'No, thanks,' Liam told him. 'I'll walk.'

His dad gave him a long look, then shrugged his shoulders as if he didn't care either way.

'Will you be home when I get back from school?' Liam asked.

'I doubt it,' his dad replied. 'There'll be lots of stuff for me to catch up with so I'm not sure what time I'll be back. You'll be OK though, won't you? Order a pizza or something.'

Liam nodded and straightened his school tie, feeling a little edgy as his dad hurried out of the room and down the stairs. Liam heard the front door slam shut. He was alone. He felt like shouting out with the exhilaration of being back on his own for the first time in days!

But he had school to get to. Liam headed down the stairs and out of the house. He locked the front door behind him, hitched his schoolbag up on to his shoulder and started walking.

Fresh air! Liam took big gasps of it. Not stuck in a hospital ward or his bedroom. But looking at everything through the dark glasses meant that it still looked as if it was twilight. He blinked hard a few times to try to clear his blurry vision. His sight wasn't going to come back straight away. Even so, Liam smiled as he saw sunlight dapple on the leaves. He noticed the white vapour trail of an aeroplane high above him in the sky. He felt as if he was seeing the world for the first time. He was grateful to be able to see anything.

'Liam.'

He heard his name shouted from behind him and turned.

'Oh no,' Liam muttered. Even with his dodgy eyesight, he could still recognize Wesley Brown and Joshua Clemence hurrying towards him.

Liam braced himself for the first jokes and insults about his large dark glasses.

'Liam, are you all right?' Wesley asked. Liam was surprised – and suspicious – to hear genuine concern in his voice. 'We didn't think you'd be back at school yet.'

'We thought they'd keep you in hospital longer because of the accident,' Josh added, and Liam could have sworn he saw a look of guilt on the boy's face.

What's going on? Liam thought. Liam looked at both

of the boys in turn, waiting for the inevitable jokes about his dark glasses.

'We thought that you might want a bit of company walking to school,' Wesley said. 'Crossing roads and stuff like that.'

'I can see to cross roads, thanks,' Liam told them.

'We'll walk with you anyway,' Josh added. 'We thought we'd walk home with you after school too. If you don't mind.'

'No, I don't mind,' Liam said, wondering if they were setting him up for some kind of practical joke.

But as the three of them walked along, Liam became more and more convinced that their concern was real.

Perhaps while he'd been in hospital having his eyes repaired, someone had repaired Wesley's and Josh's brains. Either that or they'd replaced them with robots. Liam wasn't sure what was going on.

'So what did they do to your eyes?' Josh asked as the three of them drew up to the school gates.

'Do you really want to know?' Liam grinned.

'Not if it's bloody,' Josh said. 'I hate blood.'

All three boys laughed. It felt good. It was the first time Liam had laughed in ages.

As they wandered into the school playground, Liam noticed other pupils glancing at him. But no one stared or pointed, and certainly no one made fun of him.

In fact, three people patted him encouragingly on the back as he passed them. Liam was quietly thrilled! This was the first time he'd had any proper contact with his school-mates since his mum left home. It felt weird but he was actually beginning to think that the accident might have been some sort of blessing in disguise.

'Aren't you two going off to play football?' Liam asked.

'No, we're going to stay with you until the bell goes,' Wesley told him.

'We'll meet you outside the main gates after school,' Josh told him. 'The three of us can walk home together. Did your dad tell you we were the ones who delivered your get well cards? He had a little word with us about your accident.'

Liam suddenly stopped in his tracks. He remembered his dad's threat of revenge in the hospital. What had his dad been doing?

'What did he say?' Liam asked.

'Not much,' Josh said quickly.

Liam nodded as the bell sounded to signal the start of the school day.

Wesley and Josh walked through the main doors on either side of Liam, as if they were protecting him. When they were all safely inside, Wesley put one hand on Liam's shoulder.

'See you later,' he said.

'Be careful,' Josh added. Then both boys hurried off to their own classroom.

Liam couldn't help but smile to himself as he walked towards his own class. It seemed that Wesley and Josh had stopped their teasing at last. It was just a pity that it had taken a face full of acid for that to happen. But what if his dad had had words with the boys too? Which would mean . . . which would mean that their concern wasn't real.

But Liam didn't want to think about that. He turned towards his classroom door and wondered how the rest of his class would treat him.

As Liam walked across the playground towards the school gates at the end of the day, people crowded round to wish him well. It was all becoming a little bit overwhelming. Liam was grateful for their concern but he was starting to feel like an invalid – or a school celebrity.

Wesley and Josh were waiting for him at the school gates and the three boys set off for home. Liam had to hide a smile at how many times the boys asked him if he was all right.

'Kerb coming up, Liam,' Josh said as they approached a road. Josh even offered his arm for support if Liam needed it.

'Thanks, Josh,' Liam said. 'You two have been really kind but I'll be OK getting home from here.'

'No, we'll walk with you,' Wesley told him.

Liam smiled.

'The houses where you live are really nice, aren't they?' Josh said, glancing around at some of the large properties on either side of the road. 'They must be expensive. I reckon there's a few millionaires living around here.'

'Is your dad a millionaire, Liam?' Wesley asked. 'I mean, you live in a big house.'

'My dad's not a millionaire,' Liam said, as they turned into his street. 'At least I don't think he is. Unless he's got loads of money hidden away that I don't know about.'

The other two boys laughed.

Liam looked towards the row of trees that ran the length of the road.

He stopped walking, staring at something a few metres ahead.

'What is it, Liam?' Wesley asked.

Liam didn't answer. He blinked hard and reached for his dark glasses, pulling them off to rub at his eyes.

'There's something there,' he said quietly. Whatever

it was, it made his pulse quicken. He put the glasses
back on and peered at one of the trees nearby.

'Yeah, it's a tree,' Josh chuckled.

Liam shook his head.

Is that a man standing there behind that tree?

The dark shape was the size of a man but it was
blurred so badly, Liam couldn't make out any features.
He could see arms and legs. A torso. A head. But, apart
from that, the silhouette looked like nothing more
than a sinister moving shadow. Moving towards Liam.
Liam started to back away.

'Liam?' Wesley asked, taking a step towards him.

Liam's heart was pounding hard in his chest.

The black shape lunged at him.

Liam shouted in fear and dropped to the ground,
hands covering his head to protect himself.

'What happened?' Josh asked, kneeling beside
Liam and putting a hand around his shoulder. 'What's
going on?'

'Didn't you see it?' Liam blurted out, looking up, his
breath coming in gasps.

'There's nothing there,' Wesley told him.

'It was a man,' Liam protested. 'He tried to attack me.'

'Liam, there wasn't a man there,' Josh assured him. 'We're the only ones on the street.'

Liam was breathing heavily as he got to his feet. He saw Josh and Wesley exchange a glance that clearly said they thought he was loopy.

'I saw him,' he gasped. 'I couldn't make out his face but . . .' Liam was frightened. And he had no idea how to explain what he had just seen to these two boys.

'It must be some kind of side effect from your operation,' Josh said gently. 'Your vision's not quite right yet. That's all it is, I bet.'

Liam looked up and down the street.

There was no one there. No dark shapes. Josh must be right.

You imagined it, Liam told himself. *Your eyes just aren't working properly yet. There was no one there.*

'You're right,' he said to Josh, trying to smile. 'It must be something to do with the operation.'

'Either that or you're losing the plot,' Wesley chuckled.

Josh laughed and Liam tried to join in, even though he was still shaken up.

The three boys walked on. Liam forced himself not to glance back at the tree as he passed it.

Liam dreaded the nights now.

That was when the shape came.

Over the weeks that disturbing shadow had become clearer and clearer to him as his vision returned.

His nerves were completely strung out. He never left the house after dark now and he always switched on the lights as soon as the first hint of dusk began to colour the sky.

Liam stood at the front window of the living-room, peering out into the night. His dad was out, as usual.

A car sped past, making him jump. He pulled the curtains and turned back towards the sofa where he'd been sitting watching TV.

Something moved to his right.

44

He spun round.

There was nothing there. No blurred figure of a man. No dark outline of a person standing close to him or trying to grab him.

Liam sighed, switched off the TV and decided it was time to go to bed. At least when he was asleep he was safe.

Wasn't he?

'What about the nightmares?' he asked himself. As soon as he said the words, the memories came flooding back to him.

He was being chased down a narrow dark alley in the dead of night by that same blurred figure he had seen so often out of the corner of his eye. And every time he'd been unable to make out the person's features. Anonymous, sinister . . . and after Liam.

Liam shook his head, trying to shake himself free of the vision.

Before his operation he'd hardly ever had nightmares – and could never remember them properly. Since he'd come home from hospital, he'd had more nightmares than ever before. And he could remember every dreadful detail.

It had to be something to do with the operation, he told himself, climbing the stairs and entering his bedroom. Perhaps, as time passed, the headaches and the nightmares would stop. They *had* to. He'd go mad, otherwise.

The one thing he was grateful for was that his vision had slowly improved. He glanced at the dark glasses on his bedroom desk, relieved that he didn't have to wear them any more.

Liam pulled on his pyjamas, yawning. He climbed into bed, but he could already feel the beginning of a headache building at the base of his skull. The pain seemed to move to his eyes until it felt as if someone was inside his head banging away with a sledgehammer. Liam wondered how long it would take him to drift off to sleep.

He lay on his back and stared at the ceiling, his eyes half closed. Slowly, slowly he felt himself start to fall asleep.

Something large and dark moved close to his bed.

It was the size of a man. The figure was tall and powerfully built, but the face looked like a black mask. The shadowy silhouette leaned over Liam's bed. Only the gleaming white teeth were visible in the dark lump of a head.

Liam sat up, gasping for breath, his hand flailing for his bedside lamp. In his panic he hit the light too hard and sent it crashing to the floor.

Liam swung himself quickly out of bed, going for the main light switch. If he could just turn a light on, the shadow would disappear, leaving Liam alone again.

As Liam's feet hit the floor, a shiver ran up his body. He felt something cold beneath his feet. He looked down, and was amazed to see that he wasn't standing on his bedroom carpet but on grey, damp concrete.

He felt himself trembling and wrapped his arms around himself. His thin cotton pyjamas were no protection against the cold wind that suddenly whipped around him. Liam swivelled round on the spot, taking in his surroundings. His bedroom posters had disappeared. Instead, he was surrounded by tall brick walls, oozing with damp and covered in rough graffiti.

He was in some kind of alley. Trapped in another nightmare. He could see the weak, yellow glow of streetlights at the far end, but they seemed miles away. Dustbins huddled together; some had been knocked over, spilling their reeking contents on to the wet concrete. Pieces of torn paper occasionally rose into the cold night air, tossed by the strong wind. An empty drink can rattled past Liam. All he wanted to do was get out of this horrible place and back into the warmth of his bed.

Close by, he heard footsteps. Coming towards him.

He didn't wait to see who they belonged to. He turned and started walking as quickly as he could in the opposite direction, his terror building fast. The footsteps quickened.

With dreadful certainty, Liam looked over his shoulder. He already knew he would see the shadowy outline of a man – just like in all the other nightmares.

Liam turned slowly and then let out a cry of shock. He was wrong – this nightmare wasn't the same as all the others. He started to back away as he made out the sinister outline of *three* men walking towards him. They were huge and menacing, even if he couldn't see their faces. With a shout, they broke into a run and Liam turned on his heel.

Liam ran as fast as he could, heading towards the end of the alley, but the lights in front of him never seemed to get any closer.

'It's only a dream!' he said to himself. 'Wake up! Wake up!' But his limbs were like lead and Liam couldn't struggle out of the nightmare. He had no choice. He had to keep running. But no matter how far and how fast he ran, he couldn't get out.

And, all the time, the dark shapes drew nearer. Now he could hear their panting as they gained on him.

Liam gasped as he ran. He felt as though his lungs would burst. He leaped over an overturned dustbin and dashed on, not daring to look back. He could hear the pounding footsteps getting closer.

He tripped on a cracked paving-stone and fell heavily.

As he rolled helplessly on to his back, he saw the dark shapes approaching, arms outstretched and reaching for him.

Liam shouted in terror.

He was still shouting when he woke up.

For a second he looked wildly around, trying to see the dark shapes – but the realization gradually hit him. He was in bed. He wasn't in a stinking alley with overturned dustbins and rain-soaked paving slabs.

He exhaled deeply and screwed up his eyes.

His pyjama top was drenched with sweat.

Someone opened his bedroom door. His dad stood there in his overcoat. He must have come back home while Liam was still in his nightmare.

'Liam, are you all right?' his dad asked. 'I heard you shout out.'

'It was just a nightmare,' he said. He hoped his dad wouldn't ask any questions. Liam didn't want to talk about what he'd just seen, what he'd been running away from.

His dad hesitated in the doorway for a moment, then crossed to the bed and sat down on the end of it.

'What happened?' his dad wanted to know. 'What happened in the nightmare?'

Great, Liam thought. *Now I have to live through the whole thing again.* But he knew his dad wouldn't go till he had an answer.

'I was being chased by someone,' Liam began. 'I couldn't make out who it was. I was in some kind of alley.' He wiped his face with a clammy hand. 'I've had this same nightmare before but it's never been so real. I think . . . I think someone was trying to kill me.'

His dad shifted uncomfortably on the edge of the bed. 'Why would you think that?'

I don't know,' Liam confessed. 'I've been seeing the same figure ever since my operation. It's a man, I know that. But I can't make out his face or what he's wearing. I've seen him in the street too and in the house. Or at least, I think I've seen him out of the corner of my eye. I know it sounds bizarre.'

'And all this has happened since the operation?' his

dad asked gently. Liam nodded, feeling that his dad was really listening to him. This was the longest conversation they'd had in ages.

'You can't have seen anyone in the house, Liam,' his dad said. 'I'd have seen them too. And besides, I wouldn't let anyone in here.'

'That's why I think it's something to do with the operation,' Liam continued. 'Perhaps there's still something wrong with my eyes.'

His dad shook his head.

'The operation was a success,' he said vehemently. 'The doctor told you that. The fact that you can even see should prove it to you.'

'Then why am I having these nightmares and headaches?' Liam persisted. 'Why am I seeing this figure? And why does it feel as if it's trying to get me?'

Liam's dad could only shrug his shoulders.

'What do you think it is, Liam?' he asked finally. 'The figure? The nightmare? What do you think it means?'

'I don't know,' Liam admitted.

'It couldn't be all the pressure of . . . well, you know?
Things getting to you?' his dad asked. He reached out
a hand and it hovered over one of Liam's. Then he
seemed to think better of it and grabbed his hand
back, getting up off the bed. Had he actually been
trying to comfort Liam? Understand him? But wasn't
that just typical? He couldn't see it through!

Liam swung himself out of bed and pushed past his
dad towards the bedroom door.

'Where are you going?' his dad asked.

'I'm going downstairs to get a glass of water,' Liam
said flatly.

He padded across the landing and down the stairs to
the kitchen, thoughts whirling about in his head and
the images from his nightmare still all too vivid.

Liam walked into the kitchen without switching on
the lights. The full moon, shining brightly in the night
sky, flooded the room with milky light. He crossed to
a cupboard, pulled out a glass, then went to the sink to
fill it. The water splashed noisily into the stainless-
steel sink.

He looked out of the large window that offered a view over the back garden.

The moonlight gave everything a cold white glow and Liam could see over the lawn to the pond then beyond to the hedge at the bottom of the garden.

A dark figure stepped out from behind a tree.

Liam gasped and dropped his glass into the sink where it smashed.

Liam watched as the shape ducked out of sight again.

It was the same figure he'd seen in his nightmares, Liam was sure of it.

Liam's terrified gaze fixed on that spot where he'd seen the figure, waiting for it to heave into view again. His heart was hammering against his ribs so hard it felt like it might burst out of his chest.

There was a high-pitched, rasping shriek out in the garden, somewhere to his right.

Liam's eyes darted in the direction of the shriek, then shifted back to where he'd seen the figure. He squinted out into the gloom.

More rasping shrieks came out of the garden. Couldn't his dad hear them?

What's going on? he asked himself, gripping the kitchen counter for support, trying to calm himself down.

A hand closed over his shoulder.

Liam shouted in fear and spun round to see his dad standing there.

'There's someone out there,' Liam blurted, pointing towards where he'd seen the figure. 'There's someone watching the house.'

His dad looked to where Liam was pointing.

'I can't see anything,' he said.

'That's because he's hiding behind the tree,' Liam gasped. 'I saw him.' The two of them turned to gaze out of the window.

A large black cat sauntered into view on the lawn and sat there licking one of its paws.

'That's what you saw, Liam,' his dad said. 'That cat.'

Liam shook loose from his dad's hand. 'It wasn't a cat,' he snapped. 'I know it wasn't. There was someone there.'

'The same someone you've seen in your dreams?' his dad asked.

Liam knew his dad wasn't taking him seriously. He gazed at his dad for long seconds, then turned his back and walked away.

When the final bell sounded, Liam was the first one on his feet.

As he hurried towards the door of the science lab, he saw Mr Parker watching him. The teacher beckoned to Liam.

'Liam, can I have a word, please?' Mr Parker said.

Liam sighed and wandered over to the teacher's desk while his fellow pupils pushed, barged and hurried out of the lab. Mr Parker waited for the classroom to empty.

'Is everything all right, Liam?' he asked eventually.

'Yes, thanks,' Liam assured him. 'Am I in trouble or something?'

'No,' Mr Parker smiled. 'It's just that you're usually the last one to leave, not the first. Before your accident

I couldn't get rid of you. Since your accident you can't wait to leave school every day.'

'I've things to do,' Liam said.

'Is there anything you want to tell me?' Mr Parker persisted. 'Any problems at school or at home?'

Well, I'm seeing visions of someone who's chasing me and probably trying to kill me, Liam thought to himself. Probably best not to mention that. His science teacher was hardly likely to believe in visions, was he?

'Everything's fine,' Liam told him. 'I've just got something important to do, that's all.' Liam knew he was shutting Mr Parker out when his teacher was only trying to help. But what choice did he have? His dad didn't believe him, so why should anyone else? And anyway, Liam wasn't lying. He *did* have something important to do – very important.

'OK, Liam,' Mr Parker said. 'Sorry to have kept you.'

Liam turned and almost ran out of the classroom. He hurried down the stairs to the ground floor of the school then out of the main doors and sprinted towards the bus stop.

There was a bus due any minute that would take him close to the hospital.

When the bus arrived, Liam got on, paid his fare and walked to the back. He sat gazing out of the window, his mind still reeling. His heart was thumping fast: a combination of anxiety and excitement.

If I can just find out who the donor was, he thought, *perhaps I'll be able to understand what I've been seeing.*

The bus pulled up at the stop next to the hospital. Liam jumped to his feet and hurried off. He ran towards the large building, dashing across the road behind an ambulance that pulled away with its blue lights flashing and its sirens blaring.

Liam stopped running as he got to the main doors of the hospital, taking deep breaths to compose himself. Then he walked briskly through the main entrance and along the corridor towards the lifts that would carry him to the floor and the ward he wanted.

He could still feel his heart beating fast but now it wasn't because of his running. It was nerves. With any luck, he was about to discover the identity of the cornea donor.

He pressed the button for level three. The doors quietly glided shut and the lift set off. Liam leaned back against the wall. A few seconds later the doors reopened with a ping and Liam stepped out into the corridor. The noises and smells were all too familiar. With a shudder, Liam remembered being wheeled through these corridors.

A young nurse sat behind a desk, writing on a small pad. On both sides of her there were manila files stacked high. Liam could see name tags on each of them.

Liam coughed politely into his hand.

'Can I help you?' the nurse asked, smiling.

'My name's Liam Webb,' he told her. 'I had an operation here about three weeks ago. It was a cornea transplant.'

'I hope you're feeling better now,' the nurse said.

'Oh, yes, thanks,' Liam replied. 'I was wondering if I could see the records of my operation.'

'What do you mean?' the nurse wanted to know, her smile fading slightly.

'I wanted to know who donated the corneas that I was given,' Liam told her.

The phone on her desk rang. She picked it up.

'Yes,' she said. 'Not at the moment.'

Liam sighed as he watched her. Behind him, an orderly whistled cheerfully, wheeling past a trolley of clean sheets and blankets.

'Just hang on a minute,' she said to whoever was on the other end of the line. She cupped her hand over the mouthpiece and leaned over the counter towards Liam.

'We're not allowed to give out that kind of information, I'm afraid,' she told him.

No! Liam wasn't going to give up now.

'Please, it's very important,' Liam begged.

The nurse put her finger to her lips to silence him, then went back to her phone conversation.

'I gave her the medication about half an hour ago,' she said to the caller. 'Yes. OK.' She put the phone down.

'Please,' Liam said. 'Dr Newman did the operation. Couldn't you ask him?'

'I can ask him but I know what he'll say,' the nurse insisted. 'We're not allowed to give out information about organ donors.'

Liam watched as she headed off up the corridor and turned to the left out of sight. This was his chance! He glanced about him quickly, saw that no one else was around and darted behind the nurse's desk.

Liam was relieved to see that the files on the desk were in alphabetical order. He went straight to the bottom of the second pile, looking for his name.

'Vafadari. Vernon. Watson,' he read as he looked at each file name. 'Webb.' He pulled the folder out and flipped it open. There wasn't much time. Liam could hardly believe he was doing this. He'd never committed a criminal act in his life! But there they were. Pictures of his face that had obviously been taken just after he'd been brought in with the acid burns. There were also diagrams of his head and several pages of scribbled notes.

Liam looked up anxiously to make sure that no one was coming. The corridor was empty. He bent his head back over the file, desperate to find the information he wanted. There it was! Finally. Right at the back of the file there was a name. A name he didn't recognize.

'Operation to be performed: cornea transplant,' he read aloud. 'Donor: Adam Crane.'

Liam smiled and slammed shut the file, shoving it hastily back into place among the others. Then he scuttled around to the other side of the nurse's desk and waited, his heart pounding uncontrollably.

A moment later, the young nurse returned.

'I've spoken to the consultant,' said the nurse. 'And I'm afraid we're not allowed to give you the name of the donor.'

'Oh, well,' Liam said, smiling. 'That's not a problem. Thanks for asking though.' He turned and began to walk away.

Adam Crane, he thought. Bingo!

Liam was going to find out about this man and he knew exactly where to go.

* * *

The town library stayed open late most nights during term-time.

He was sure that he would find the answers he sought in there.

As he walked through the doors he could see that the large building was all but deserted. There was an old lady browsing the shelves of horror books but, other than that, the two members of staff on duty were the only people present.

Liam crossed to the enquiries desk where a tall, bald man in a pair of faded jeans and a black T-shirt stood stamping newly returned books.

'Excuse me,' Liam said. 'I need to see some back copies of the local papers.'

The man looked at him and smiled.

'We don't keep copies,' he said. 'They take up too much room. We've got all the local stuff on disk though. If you know which issue you're looking for, I can point you in the right direction.'

'All I've got is a name,' Liam shrugged. 'Adam Crane.'

'You could try the internet,' the librarian said. 'Use one of the library computers. If you put the name Adam Crane into a search engine, then it should give you what you're looking for.'

'Thanks,' Liam said and wandered over to the row of PCs that were in the reference area.

He tapped in the name Adam Crane and clicked on the 'search' icon.

Liam groaned as the search threw up thousands of results. He began scrolling through them, seeing that they covered everything from Adam and Eve in the Bible to a local crane company. But Liam was determined to find out the history behind the corneas he'd been given. He wasn't going to give up now. He started to go through each link, one by one.

As he reached the sixteenth search result, he saw what he wanted. Liam clicked on it. It was a page from the local newspaper. There was even a picture of Adam Crane. Liam read the headline:

LOCAL MAN MURDERED

He sucked in a sharp breath and scanned the rest of the article.

Adam Crane, a thirty-five-year-old man, was beaten and left for dead in an alley early yesterday morning.

He was first believed to have been the victim of a mugging but police later revealed that Mr Crane, who had a number of previous criminal convictions, is believed to have been murdered by business associates.

It is the third such killing in the town during the last year and police say that Mr Crane's killers are more than likely professional criminals, probably the same men responsible for the previous two murders. Mr Crane worked at the town's greyhound track.

Liam noticed that there was a photograph of the murder scene. He felt the hairs on the back of his neck rise. He recognized that place. The high brick walls. The overturned rubbish bins.

It was the place he'd seen in his nightmares.

Liam looked at the date on the paper cutting.

He swallowed hard.

Adam Crane had been murdered less than a month earlier. Liam sat back in his seat, his eyes still fixed on the computer screen. So, Liam finally knew what had happened to the man whose corneas had been donated to him. A criminal, murdered by other criminals. And in the same alley Liam had seen in his nightmares.

What does it mean? Liam asked himself. *Is this man's death appearing in my dreams?* Liam felt beads of sweat on his forehead. He suddenly jumped to his feet, the chair clattering to the floor behind him, and ran out of the library.

All he wanted to do was get home.

As he turned into the street, Liam was relieved to see his dad's car parked in the driveway.

Still panting from the long run from the library, Liam pushed through the front door and towards the living-room, where he could hear the sound of the television.

His dad looked round as Liam entered the room.

'Are you all right?' he asked, seeing how breathless and pale Liam looked. 'I wondered where you were.'

'I went to the hospital first, then to the library,' Liam said, flopping down in the chair opposite his dad. 'I told you I needed to find out the name of the cornea donor.'

'And did you?' his dad asked, sounding genuinely interested.

'His name was Adam Crane,' Liam said.

He saw the expression on his dad's face darken. He leaned forward in his chair, as if keen to hear more, but he didn't say anything.

'It said in the local paper that he was murdered,' Liam continued. 'It said that he was a criminal, that he was probably murdered by other criminals. It didn't say why though.'

His dad threw himself back in the chair, fingers drumming on the arm.

'It said that he worked at the local greyhound track,' Liam said. 'You own that track, don't you, Dad? He must have worked for you. Did you know him?'

Liam's dad shook his head.

'And the weirdest thing of all is that he was killed in the same alleyway that I keep dreaming about,' Liam went on. 'It's like I'm seeing through his eyes what happened to him.'

Liam's dad said nothing. But Liam couldn't stop talking. Now that he'd found out who the donor was, he had to get the story out – tell it to someone. Even if it was his dad.

'He's the man I've been seeing in my visions,' Liam panted. 'Him and the blokes who killed him.'

'Visions?' his dad said. 'What you've been having aren't visions. You've had a couple of bad dreams and that's it. If I were you I'd get something to eat and then go to bed. Forget about this Adam Crane bloke and about what you read.'

'But I thought you'd want to know!' Liam protested. 'He was murdered and—'

'And nothing, Liam,' his dad snapped, turning his attention back to the TV screen.

Liam hesitated a moment, then got to his feet and

padded towards the living-room door.

'And don't tell anyone about Crane or what you read,' his dad said irritably. 'People will get fed up with you and all this attention seeking.'

Liam thought about arguing but he knew it would be useless. He should have known better than to confide in his dad.

He went to his bedroom and pulled on his pyjamas quickly, wanting nothing more than to sleep. He'd lost any appetite he might have had. As soon as he climbed into bed, he could feel himself sinking deeper and deeper into unconsciousness. His body welcomed it. He was gone . . .

He felt a cold breeze ruffle his hair and, as he looked around, he saw the tall brick walls on either side of him and the overturned dustbins. Liam shuddered. He was no longer in his bedroom. He was back in the alley again.

As he hurried down the alley, he felt the wind whipping around him. That old, familiar cold seeping into his bones.

He turned as he heard the footsteps.

A large, familiar black shape loomed into view. The same panic flooded Liam's veins.

Liam began to run.

The figure ran after him.

Liam prayed he would wake up. He knew he was dreaming, knew that this dream was about Adam Crane. Nothing to do with him! He knew that, any second, he would sit up in bed, sweating and terrified. But he couldn't stop running. Behind him, his shadowy pursuers chased after him.

Liam tripped and almost fell.

He pulled himself up and ran on, his heart hammering hard against his ribs.

He blinked hard, looking for the streetlights ahead of him, but they had disappeared. He could only see blackness. And out of that blackness came three more shapes.

Liam skidded to a halt. He was trapped. He could smell the stench of rotting food and litter all around him. The bare brick walls looked greasy, as if they were sweating. Liam could feel the claustrophobic narrowness of the alley crush in upon him. Above him, he could see the dark and seething night sky. Liam felt as if it was pushing down on him, making it difficult to move.

He heard a dog howl madly.

Terrified, he looked at the walls on either side of him, wondering if he could scramble up them to escape.

He was still gazing up at the walls when he felt a powerful punch to his face.

The blow split his bottom lip; blood burst from the savage cut and spilled down his chin as he hit the ground hard, scraping his palms on the rough and reeking concrete.

Liam felt a kick to his ribs. Then another and another and suddenly, all he knew was pain. Fists and boots were raining down on him. He tasted more blood in his mouth.

He screamed for help. Or Adam Crane screamed. Liam couldn't be sure who he was any more.

'Leave him.'

Liam looked up, wiping blood from his face.

As the hammer of kicks and punches halted, Liam could see another figure walking towards him through the darkness.

The figure stopped a couple of metres away. Liam could see his face and felt his stomach shrink to a tight knot inside him.

'You just couldn't let it go, could you?' said the man. 'I warned you.'

Liam shook his head in horror, not wanting to believe what he saw.

'It's me! Liam!' he shouted out. 'I'm not who you think I am.'

The figure stepped closer. It was clear that he couldn't hear what Liam was saying.

'You kept sticking your nose in where it wasn't wanted,' he said. 'And now you'll have to pay.'

Liam looked in terror at the snarling face. At the huge frame of the man who leaned over him.

The man curled his lip fiercely. Then Liam saw the

scar on his neck. Now there was no mistaking who the gang leader was.

'Oh no,' Liam gasped. 'No.' Liam knew what was going to happen. He'd already read about it in the newspaper article. Even though this time it was happening inside Liam's dream, he didn't seem to have any power to stop it.

'NO,' Liam screamed.

The man shook his head scornfully.

His dad stepped back, motioning the dark shapes all around Liam forward.

'Finish it,' his dad said quietly.

Liam screamed as he felt more kicks and punches hammering into him. His entire body was racked with pain.

All that was left was darkness.

FROZEN IN TIME

'The famous wax museum,' Harry Ash grinned as he looked at the billboard above the main entrance of the building. Then he nodded towards the old woman sitting in the ticket kiosk. 'Reckon she's a waxwork?' he asked. 'She hasn't moved for five minutes.'

His three friends all laughed.

'Who do you think that's supposed to be?' Lucy Nash asked, pointing at one of the faces on the billboard.

'Someone out of a rock band, though I'm not sure which,' Harry laughed. Harry was a music fanatic, so if he couldn't recognize the waxwork – well, that said it all.

'What about that one?' Anna asked, pointing at another.

'That's either Henry the Eighth or that bloke who plays for Chelsea,' Nick said.

Some of their other classmates joined in the laughter as they studied the billboards and the entrance to the wax museum.

'COME AND SEE THE STARS OF TELEVISION AND FILMS' boasted one of them. Beneath it was a drawing of the Oscar statuette with various faces around it.

'MIX WITH THE SPORTING GREATS' a billboard on the other side of the entrance offered. There were pictures of footballers, boxers, runners and other athletes in various poses.

'All right, come on, everyone. Line up.'

Mr Taylor fumbled with his glasses as he called out

to the class. He was a supply teacher, and possibly the most nervous one Harry and his friends had ever had. They joined their classmates in a reasonably orderly line on the pavement outside the entrance to the wax museum.

'Come on,' Mr Taylor called again. 'I need to count you all in. I don't want anyone sneaking off while we're inside.'

'There's got to be some joke we can play on Taylor while we're here,' Lucy whispered to Anna. Harry and Nick could both hear what she'd said. Harry nudged Nick and smiled.

'Right,' Mr Taylor continued. 'If you go through two at a time. Just walk up to the main door and wait there for me.'

The class began moving towards the entrance.

'Two, four, six,' Mr Taylor counted as they passed him.

Harry, Nick, Lucy and Anna reached the teacher.

'Wait, wait, everyone,' Mr Taylor called. 'I've lost count.'

'He's the worst supply teacher we've ever had,' Lucy muttered.

'Oh, come on, Lucy,' Harry said. 'He's not that bad. I mean, he's brought us here for the day.'

'Well, unless he learns how to count, we're never going to get inside,' Lucy grunted.

'OK, let's start again,' Mr Taylor said. 'When you get inside just wait in the hallway until I tell you to move.'

'Shall we stay still, sir?' asked one of Harry's classmates.

'Yes, yes. That's right,' said Mr Taylor gratefully. Harry could see what was coming next.

'Like a waxwork?' asked the same pupil.

Groaning at the bad joke, everyone started walking past Mr Taylor into the wax museum. Just before Harry walked through the large brass doors, he peered inside the ticket kiosk. The old lady still hadn't moved a muscle.

'She *must* be made of wax!' Harry said.

The old lady jerked her head in his direction and scowled.

'Maybe not,' Harry added under his breath.

* * *

'Right, everyone. Listen to me,' Mr Taylor called, raising both his hands above his head for silence.

Harry and the rest of his class stopped chattering. On either side of them the walls were covered by dusty black curtains. Harry looked up and saw that the ceiling was also painted black. He could smell something like damp wood. It was a fusty smell that stuck in his nostrils. To his left he saw a faded cardboard cut-out of someone he didn't recognize. The floor beneath his feet, he noticed, was visible in several places through the threadbare carpet. The museum had definitely seen better days.

'We're going to make our way to the first exhibit now,' the teacher announced. 'I want you all to stay close to me and no talking. Unless you've got a question about the exhibits. And,' he added as an afterthought, 'no wandering off on your own.'

Harry again looked at Nick who nodded. They both knew exactly what the other was thinking. That's what

Harry liked about Nick – they shared the same evil streak.

But when Harry looked round, he saw that Lucy was watching them, her hands on her hips. She stepped between the two boys.

'What are you two laughing about?' she demanded.

'You'll see,' Harry told her, grinning. 'Come on, let's see what the models look like.'

Harry and the others walked down a narrow corridor. Harry tried not to notice the musty smell that followed them everywhere.

'Oi, Mark, over here,' Harry heard someone call.

'All right, keep it down,' Mr Taylor shouted. 'This is a waxworks *museum*, not an amusement park. Try to behave a bit better. There are other members of the public in here too, you know.'

No one took any notice. The floorboards creaked in protest as everyone clattered down the corridor, whooping out remarks and insults to each other. Harry saw Mr Taylor throw his hands in the air helplessly.

'Don't worry about it, sir,' Harry told him, as he

walked past. 'We don't take much notice of any of our teachers.' Mr Taylor smiled weakly.

As Harry walked further down the corridor, it became darker and darker. The walls here were also painted black and ancient light fittings gave out a dull yellow light. The floor was carpeted with ancient tiles that curled up at the corners and dust-balls scudded across the floor. The walls were lined with ancient posters, cracked with age. Harry felt as though he were walking into a mausoleum rather than a waxwork museum.

'I wish I'd brought a torch,' Harry heard someone call out. But their voice sounded anxious rather than amused.

'Calm down,' Mr Taylor said.

Finally, the corridor opened up and with a sense of relief Harry stepped into an exhibition room.

'Thank goodness for that,' Lucy said, shivering. Harry knew exactly what she meant.

The first exhibit looked like a massive three-dimensional painting. Set behind a huge piece of polished glass, it was a reconstruction of a meeting room in a Victorian house. There was a long wooden table in the middle of the exhibit and all around it were various figures from history.

'Ooh, the excitement is too much!' said Nick. But he still joined the rest of the class as they gathered around to look. Harry could see a figure of Napoleon standing beside Nelson and the Duke of Wellington. Next to them was a waxwork of Winston Churchill leaning over a map with Nelson Mandela, while Adolf Hitler looked on. At the far end of the table sat models of the current American President and the British Prime Minister. Fortunately, there were name-plates in front of each figure. Otherwise, Harry wasn't sure he'd have recognized any of them.

'That has got to be the most bizarre collection of people,' Anna said, as she stood on tiptoes to read the name-plates. 'I mean, what kind of a warped mind puts Adolf Hitler next to Nelson Mandela!'

'Hold me down,' Harry whispered to Nick. 'I don't think I can keep still from the excitement.'

'Right, everyone, you can see that these are all great leaders from the past and present,' Mr Taylor said. 'Either military or political.'

'Where's Michael Jackson?' someone asked.

'Michael Jackson isn't a world leader,' Mr Taylor sighed.

The rest of the class laughed.

'Now, who knows which country Napoleon was Emperor of?' their teacher asked.

Before anyone had a chance to answer, the piercing jingle of a mobile phone started to play. It was the type of irritating ringtone that had gone out of fashion years ago. There was only one person who that phone could possibly belong to.

Mr Taylor muttered something under his breath and fumbled in his pocket for the phone. He wandered away from the group as he pulled the phone from his jacket pocket.

'I'll be back in a minute,' he called. 'All of you just stay where you are.'

'Now's our chance,' Harry said quietly.

'Chance for what?' Anna wanted to know.

'The chance to make this visit a lot more interesting,' Harry told her as he and Nick stepped back into the shadows away from the exhibit and the rest of the class.

'Is this what you two were on about earlier?' Lucy asked.

'If you're skiving off, you're not going without us,' said Anna. 'It was Lucy and I who thought of playing a trick on Mr Taylor in the first place.'

Lucy nodded.

'That's right,' she reminded Harry, readjusting the band on her ponytail. 'So if you two are going somewhere, so are we. Anyway, you two will get scared on your own.'

'In your dreams,' Nick grunted.

'We're not skiving off,' Harry told her. 'We're going to go round the other way. We'll go round in reverse and meet everyone else in the middle. Can you imagine the look on Mr Taylor's face?' Anna and Lucy looked at each other and then broke into matching grins.

'Yes!' cheered Nick, punching the air.

'Quiet,' Anna said, grabbing his arm. 'We don't want everyone to hear.'

'Yes,' Lucy added. 'We don't want anyone from our class seeing us either.'

'Come on then,' Harry urged. 'Let's get moving before Mr Taylor finishes his phone call. He won't even notice we're gone.'

'Just back away,' Nick whispered. 'Come on.'

Moving as if they were part of the shadows, they tiptoed backwards away from their classmates.

'What if someone sees us?' Lucy murmured.

'They won't,' Harry assured her. 'It's too dark.'

Anna had to stifle a giggle. Harry felt his heart thumping harder with excitement.

This is going to be wicked, Harry thought.

The four of them moved away unnoticed by anyone, into the gloom of the next corridor.

'Free!' Harry exclaimed loudly, raising his hands in the air to celebrate.

'Free to roam,' Nick echoed, smiling.

Anna and Lucy gave small whoops of delight and spun round and round in exhilaration.

'Mr Taylor would have gone mad if he'd seen us sneaking off,' Anna grinned as she stumbled to a stop.

'Not as mad as he'll go when he sees us coming the other way to meet him,' Harry assured her.

Harry counted just five other visitors to the wax museum as he and his three friends made their way in reverse down the corridor. He smiled to himself at the bemused expressions on the tourists' faces as they clearly wondered what these four friends in school uniform were doing walking the *wrong* way.

'What's going on?' Harry heard one man whisper to his wife. 'Are we meant to go round all this *twice*?'

The four of them wandered down the corridor, lazily ducking their heads into rooms and laughing at the exhibits. Every waxwork was as bad as the next. It was unbelievable just how pathetic one museum could be.

'And to think our parents paid for this!' snorted Nick.

They stepped into another room where there was a tableau called ISTANBUL 2005. It showed the Liverpool football team lifting the European Cup. Harry raised his thumb in salute as they passed it.

He noticed that the next part of the museum had no glass panels in front of the figures. All that separated the wax models from the visitors was a low rope barrier.

Harry paused before a figure of Elvis Presley and gave him an ironic hip-swivel salute.

'Wow, look at that one,' he said, grinning as he approached a figure of Britney Spears. The waxwork was dressed in ripped jeans, cowboy boots and a tattered black T-shirt. A crude blonde wig sat at a rakish angle on the waxwork's head and monstrous false eyelashes made her look more like a drag queen than a pop princess. The waxwork didn't even have Britney's famous pierced belly-button!

'It doesn't look like her at all,' Lucy grinned. 'Mind you, none of the other figures look like who they're supposed to be either.'

'Come on,' Harry protested sarcastically. 'There's got to be a hint of Britney in there. I'll take a closer look.' The others watched as he leaped over the rope barrier and marched over to stare straight into the waxwork's face.

'Come back!' protested Anna, looking over her shoulder. 'You'll get into trouble!'

Harry shook his head at Anna. 'That's the whole point, Anna. You can't get into trouble with Taylor. He wouldn't know *how* to tell us off. We can do what we like.' His friends laughed nervously as they realized he was right. Harry turned back round to the waxwork.

'Hi, Britney,' he said, smiling. 'Want to dance with me?'

The other three laughed.

'That's the closest you're ever going to get to Britney Spears, Harry,' Lucy teased.

Harry reached out one hand and touched the rough blonde wig. It shifted slightly under the weight of his hand. He gazed deeply into the dull glaze of the waxwork's brown eyes.

'What are you doing on Friday night?' Harry asked. 'Fancy coming out with me? We could go to a burger place. Then I'll take you to the cinema, if you like.' He softly stroked the figure's cheek with one hand, feeling the cold wax beneath his fingers. Then he leaned in closer, pretending to kiss it.

That's when it happened. As he drew close, the waxwork's eyes flickered in his direction.

Harry shouted in surprise and jumped away. He stumbled backwards, tripping over the low rope barrier and falling to the ground, his arms wheeling as he tried to save himself.

'What happened?' Nick asked, laughing. He reached down a hand and pulled Harry back to his feet. Anna and Lucy gathered round Harry, looking at him as though he was deranged.

'Her eyes moved!' Harry said, pointing accusingly at the waxwork. It sounded stupid when he said it out loud, but something had definitely happened. He couldn't stop staring at the waxwork. Britney Spears had never seemed so spooky.

Nick, Anna and Lucy burst out laughing and Nick gave Harry a mock punch on the arm.

'Come on, mate. You're imagining things,' Nick said.

'I swear,' Harry insisted, his hands shaking. 'Her eyes moved. She looked at me.'

'Of course she did, Harry,' Lucy smiled.

'Her eyes couldn't have moved,' Anna added. 'She's made of wax. Her eyes are made of glass.'

Harry was still breathing heavily but his heartbeat was starting to slow down. He tried a smile.

'I fooled you, didn't I?' he said, as convincingly as he could. 'I just thought I'd scare you. Make you think she was alive.'

'We'd all better have a look, then,' Lucy said, stepping over the low barrier. She moved close to the Britney Spears figure and stared into its eyes. Nick and Anna joined her and Harry watched as the three of them peered at Britney's face. Anna reached out a tentative hand to touch Britney's nose.

'It's chipped!' she said, laughing.

'No eye movement here, Harry,' Nick called over his shoulder. 'Not a flicker.'

'Gotcha,' Harry said. His friends wandered away from the waxwork back to Harry.

'You were imagining things,' Lucy told him.

'I was messing about to scare you,' Harry insisted.

'You were the one who was scared,' Nick said. Harry didn't argue back. He knew Nick wouldn't let it drop until Harry admitted he was right. It wasn't worth pursuing – not if Harry wanted to save face.

'You should stop fantasizing, Harry,' Anna told him. 'The only way that Britney Spears would give you the eye is in your dreams.'

They all laughed and moved on towards the next part of the museum. Harry followed, but before he walked out of the room he glanced back one final time at the Britney Spears figure.

Its cold, lifeless eyes seemed fixed on him.

He hurried along to catch up with his friends.

* * *

'I wonder if Mr Taylor's noticed that we're gone yet?' Harry said as they climbed the staircase to the next floor of the waxwork museum.

'My one regret is that we won't be there to see the look on his face when he realizes what's happened,' said Lucy.

'Don't worry,' said Anna, as she checked her mobile for text messages. 'Half the class are there to report back. We'll hear all about it.'

The others laughed.

On either side of the narrow staircase there were ghoulish wax heads in glass cases. Each one had a metal plaque on it bearing a name.

'Which band are this lot from?' Nick wanted to know, gesturing at the heads. 'I don't recognize any of them.'

'Fool! They're people who were executed during the French Revolution,' Anna told him. 'It says so on the wall.'

'Are you sure?' Harry asked. 'I mean, the model making in here is so bad they could be members of a rock band.'

'At least none of their eyes are moving,' teased Anna.

'I told you, I was just winding you lot up,' Harry protested.

'Whatever!' the two girls said in unison.

They reached the top of the stairs. There were rooms to their right and left.

'Let's go this way,' Harry said, heading towards the right.

A large sign above the entrance announced: 'YOU TOO CAN BE A STAR'.

'Come on,' Harry urged. 'This should be good.'

A figure of a pirate stood close to the entrance. His cutlass gleamed in the bright lights above the other exhibits.

'Have your picture taken with the stars,' Harry read out loud as he stood in front of another tableau featuring the stars of a US television comedy series.

There was a large camera contraption set up in front of the wax figures.

'You put your money in here,' Harry read out, indicating a slot in the top of the metal box. 'And you can get your picture taken with the cast.'

'Wicked,' Lucy said, hurrying towards the red sofa where four of the figures were seated. 'I love that programme.'

'Me too,' added Anna, running to sit on the other end of the sofa. 'Put the money in, then, Harry.'

Harry dug in his pocket and found a pound coin. He'd been hoping to buy an ice cream later, but he guessed it would be worth it to get the photo taken. A memento of their day of rebellion.

'Ready?' he called to the two girls.

'I think he's really fit,' said Lucy, snuggling up closer to the waxwork figure of her favourite actor from the show. 'Well, in real life anyway,' she giggled, glancing at the waxen features. She slipped her own hand into the hand of the figure and rested her head against his immobile shoulder.

'Are you getting in the photo?' Harry asked Nick, who had come to stand next to him. Nick shook his head firmly.

'No way! I don't have a crush on those actors.'

Neither did Harry. He was happy to let the two girls have their photo taken without him or Nick.

'Say "Rubbish waxworks",' Harry smiled and dropped the money into the slot.

There was a whirring sound from the metal box then a bright flash.

Lucy screamed.

She jumped away from the figure she'd sat next to.

'What's wrong, Lucy?' Nick asked. 'Never had your picture taken before?'

Lucy didn't answer. She was still gazing at the wax figure, her breath coming in gasps. Anna jumped to her feet and went to her friend. Lucy looked terrified. Harry noticed that she was rubbing the palm of the hand she'd been holding the waxwork figure's hand with.

There was a whirring sound from the camera and a Polaroid photograph came out.

'I think you and Anna look more like dummies than the waxworks do,' Nick said, looking over Harry's shoulder as the photo slowly developed.

'Let's go,' Anna said, walking towards the next room. Nick followed close behind. Harry and Lucy were left alone in the room.

Lucy still stood motionless, staring at the wax figure. She held her hand up to her chest, pressing it tight.

'What's wrong, Lucy?' Harry asked quietly.

Lucy shook her head.

She reached out and stroked the cold wax cheek of the figure she'd been seated next to.

'I could have sworn . . .' she muttered to herself.

'Lucy?' Harry persisted.

'You know you said that the eyes on that Britney Spears model looked at you, Harry?' she said, still staring glassily at the figure on the sofa.

Harry nodded.

'Well, I . . .' Lucy sucked in a breath, finding it difficult to finish the sentence. 'Just as the camera flashed, I felt my hand being squeezed by that waxwork.' She nodded again towards the figure.

Harry said nothing. He didn't know what to say. But he had a strong feeling Lucy was telling the truth.

'Don't say anything to the others, will you?' she asked. 'They won't believe us.'

Harry shook his head slowly.

Lucy managed a smile then turned to follow Nick and Anna. 'Come on, let's go.'

Harry hesitated for a moment, peering closely at the figure Lucy had been sitting next to.

He walked over and touched the face of the waxwork – clammy, cold wax. He hesitated.

Then he slipped his own hand into the figure's grasp.

It felt warm and moist. Like flesh.

He pulled his hand away quickly. Then he hurried out of the room after his friends.

Another flight of stairs led Harry and his three friends down again. This time, the wooden flight was so narrow that if they reached out their arms they could touch both walls at the same time. Harry was glad of the handrail, because the steps were so narrow and winding.

When they finally reached the bottom he found

himself standing on a cold concrete floor. The air smelled damp.

It was that cloying, fusty smell that reminded Harry of drying clothes.

To the left was a well-lit area that contained various electronic games. Straight ahead there was another short flight of steps leading down to what looked like complete darkness. In fact, the blackness was so total that Harry was beginning to wonder if they would be able to go any further without a torch. There was a sign on the wall beside this entrance that read:

IT IS RECOMMENDED THAT YOUNG CHILDREN OR THOSE OF A NERVOUS DISPOSITION LEAVE NOW.

Harry took a step closer to the top of the stairs and peered down.

There were five stone steps leading down to a concrete floor and a narrow stone corridor. The smell of damp and rot seemed to waft from the doorway as if expelled from putrid lungs. There was a sign just inside the doorway, suspended from the ceiling by two rusty chains. Harry read it aloud.

' "Abandon hope all ye who enter here",' he said. If it was meant to be funny, it wasn't making Harry laugh.

'What is it?' Lucy asked, wrinkling her nose at the smell.

'It's the Chamber of Horrors,' said Harry, raising his eyebrows.

'Oh, wow,' Nick smiled. 'This should be good.'

'Yeah, really frightening, I'll bet,' Anna added. 'Not.'

They set off down the steps, enveloped by the thick blackness.

Harry thought it was like stepping into empty space. He couldn't see his feet beneath him, it was so dark. He steadied himself against the wall, recoiling slightly as he felt the moistness of the stone.

There was a stone archway just ahead and, beyond it, the light was a little brighter.

'Come on,' Nick urged. Harry hurried to follow.

Nick stepped through the archway, turning to face his friends. Harry could see that Nick looked as jittery as he felt.

A monstrous roar filled the underground chamber.

Harry couldn't help jumping slightly. Even Nick let out a yelp of surprise and fear. The girls looked deathly pale.

Nick swivelled round to see where the deafening sound had come from.

'Down there,' said Harry, pointing to a blinking red light just inside the archway. He knelt beside it and waved his hand before it.

The fiendish roar sounded again.

'It must be some kind of electric eye,' Harry smiled. 'When you walked past it, you set it off, Nick.'

'I knew that,' Nick said, trying to sound brave again.

The others followed him into the Chamber of Horrors, careful to step over the flickering electric eye so they didn't trigger the sound again.

Harry straightened up and looked round at the waxworks.

Some were imprisoned behind fake iron bars, others crouched by headstones in a graveyard setting. Harry could see Dracula lying in his coffin. Two ghouls, holding what were presumably meant to be human bones, knelt over him. Slightly further back, two of Dracula's brides stood looking on with bulging eyes, huge fangs gleaming in their blood-smeared mouths.

Frankenstein's monster was clinging to some iron bars in one corner of the room.

A witch, complete with broomstick, was suspended from the ceiling.

Close to the Frankenstein's monster's cage, a werewolf crouched ready to spring.

'He looks like your dog, Lucy,' Nick laughed, pointing at the hairy figure. Nick walked up to the werewolf figure and clicked his fingers at it. 'Here, boy,' he called mockingly.

The others laughed.

Nick stepped into the setting and stood behind the werewolf. He started barking then howling while Harry and the others also hurried into the mock graveyard.

Anna and Lucy both cackled like witches.

'I'm going to turn you into a frog, Harry,' Lucy hissed, pointing at him.

Harry grinned and walked past a grave where a zombie was pushing its way through the earth. He wandered further down the room and turned a corner.

A tall figure in a long black cape and a top hat reared over him. The figure was holding a huge knife in one hand. Harry let out an involuntary yell of alarm.

He looked down at the name-plate in front of the figure: 'JACK THE RIPPER'.

The model of the murderer was standing in a recess in the wall and Harry realized that there was room for him to squeeze in behind it. If he could do that, he could bring the waxwork model to life and scare the living daylights out of his friends!

He slipped behind the model and tried not to sneeze at the thick layer of dust that covered the waxwork's cloak. The faded linen was stiff and musty, and Harry didn't really want to touch it. But he was sure it would be worth it! He pulled the cloak around himself, satisfied that his friends wouldn't be able to see him. He had to bite his lip to stop himself laughing.

'Anna,' he said loudly, in his best spooky voice. 'Lucy. I have come for you. Come and face me if you dare.'

Through the folds of the dusty cloak, he saw the two girls share a wry glance and then start to approach the figure.

'That's gross,' said Anna, pointing at the severed head in the waxwork's hand.

'Anna,' Harry rasped. 'You will be next.'

Anna screamed at the top of her voice, her eyes bulging as she pointed at the waxwork. Harry's laugh died in his throat. He knew Anna hadn't spotted him, but something about the waxwork had terrified her.

Harry fought his way out from beneath the cloak, panic rising in his chest. He stumbled out from behind the waxwork, cobwebs and dust clinging to him.

'What's wrong?' he gasped, grabbing her by

the arms. But Anna pulled herself free and started laughing.

'Fooled you!' she said. 'We can all play practical jokes.'

'Did you think we'd fall for that?' Lucy giggled. 'We knew it was your voice, Harry.'

Harry shook his head, and let out a sigh of relief.

Nick ran round the corner and, letting out a whoop, grabbed hold of Lucy's hand, dragging her behind him as they sped into the next room. Harry and Anna broke into a run themselves and careered into the others as they burst into the room. Nick and Lucy were staring up at the sole waxwork in the room: a mummy.

Nick began dancing around in front of the bandaged figure. He backed into its arms.

'Help me, help me,' he called in mock terror. 'He's got me.'

Nick was getting way over-the-top, whipping from one side to the other as he pretended to wrestle free of the mummy's grip. He was in danger of knocking the waxwork down. But that didn't explain what Harry saw next. As Nick threw himself forwards in a fake lurch to escape, Harry saw the mummy move. A bandaged hand reached out – Harry definitely saw that.

'Nick, look out!' he shouted, stepping forward. Nick looked up sharply, catching the urgency in Harry's voice. This was no joke.

The bandaged figure lurched angrily towards Nick who spun round just in time and leaped out of the way. The waxwork froze and started to fall towards the floor. Harry caught it just in time.

'Help me, then,' he grunted to the others, trying to lever the waxwork back into position. Nick and the girls crowded round to help. They were all surprised at how heavy the waxwork was.

'I thought these figures were hollow,' Harry said, wiping his hands together.

'Help me,' came the reply. All four friends froze. None of them had said a word.

Harry felt a shiver run the full length of his spine. The hairs at the back of his neck rose.

'What did you say, Harry?' Nick asked, looking at his friend.

'I didn't say anything,' Harry said. Nick tried a laugh. It didn't sound very convincing.

'We must be imagining things,' Anna offered.

'Like Harry imagined Britney Spears's eyes moving?' Lucy said.

'The mummy said "Help me",' Harry said. He knew they'd all heard it.

Nick moved back to the bandaged figure and put his ear close to its mouth. He shook his head. Nothing.

Harry did the same.

Not a word.

'Perhaps there's some kind of electric eye on the figure,' Harry offered. 'You know, like there was at the entrance to the chamber that triggered that roaring.'

Nick nodded slowly, his gaze still fixed on the waxwork.

'Yes, that must be it,' he agreed, walking away.

Harry hesitated for a moment, his heart beating quicker.

I saw a waxwork's eyes move, he thought. *Lucy felt one squeeze her hand and now we've all heard one speak.*

Their adventure in the museum didn't feel like so much fun any more. Harry had to get his friends out of here. But how – without completely spooking them out? He had to think of a way.

'Wait for me!' he called after them, running out of the room.

'We must have seen most of it by now,' Harry said. 'Let's get out of this place and find a café in town. We can meet the others at the exit when they come out.'

The four of them were walking along a long empty corridor towards a door that Harry guessed must lead them into another part of the wax museum. There must be an emergency exit somewhere close by – there had to be. He had to get them out of here. But Lucy was already approaching another exhibition room.

'What do you think is in here?' she asked, reaching out a hand to the door. Harry had to bite his lip not to call out to her to stop. He didn't want any more surprises in this place. He didn't want to *be* in this place any more.

Lucy pulled the handle.

The door didn't move.

She tried again.

'It must be locked,' she said, turning away. Harry quietly breathed a sigh of relief.

'We'll have to go back the way we came,' Harry said. 'I'm sure there was an emergency exit back there. We can sneak out.' The four of them turned to head back along the corridor.

They'd barely started to walk away when Harry heard a creaking noise behind them. A knot of dread filled his stomach. He didn't want to turn round and look, but the others already had.

'Hey, look!' Harry heard Anna say. He turned round. The door had creaked open. Harry and the others watched as she walked towards it. Anna pushed the door wider open, the hinges screeching. Light poured out of the room and lit up Anna's face. She broke into a wide smile and caught her breath in a gasp of amazement.

'Oh, wow,' Anna whispered. Lucy came up behind her and peered into the room over Anna's shoulder.

'Wicked,' Lucy added.

'Come on, Harry,' Nick said, going to join the two girls.

Harry's legs refused to work. He stared after his friends. An overwhelming feeling of foreboding enveloped him. If only he could get everyone away from here! But the others had already gone into the room. He could hear them calling out and exclaiming. He had no choice. He had to follow. Bunching his hands together in fists, he forced himself to take a step forward. To step into the room.

Harry looked around in amazement. A million different Harrys were reflected back at him from the silver walls and metallic floor tiles.

'Check it out!' chorused the girls. A thick silver cloth hung across the canopied ceiling. The whole room was magical – but the quietness was unnerving. It was like the calm before the storm. As if the room was waiting for something to happen. The door creaked shut behind Harry and with a soft click they were cut off from the rest of the museum.

Harry walked slowly round the room, his friends silently gazing around themselves too. Nick let out a low, impressed whistle. In the middle of the room was a giant silver throne. Harry guessed that it was big enough to seat several people. All four of them would have no trouble getting on it if they wanted to and it looked as if they'd still have room to spare.

There were tables draped with silver cloths on three sides of the room, each groaning under the weight of heavy silver platters. On each of those platters was food: cream cakes, smoked salmon, cold meats, bowls of fruit, large bottles of grape juice.

'Well, if this is the staff canteen then I want a job here,' said Nick, smiling.

'There aren't any waxworks,' said Harry quietly.

'Perhaps it's not part of the main exhibition,' Anna offered, looking hungrily at the food.

'It could be for some kind of photo-shoot or something,' Lucy suggested. 'Maybe some celebrities are coming here. Real ones.'

Harry looked around the room, running a hand through his hair.

'I don't think we should touch anything,' he said. 'I mean, all this food and drink is fresh so that probably means it was put here recently. Whoever put it here might be back soon. I think we should just go.' His reasoning sounded pathetic even to him. But he had to get everyone out of this room!

The others hesitated.

'Come on,' Harry insisted, his voice catching. He strode towards the door and tried to open it. But the handle didn't budge. He shook it angrily and tried again. Nothing.

'It's locked!' he said, panic flooding his veins. He threw himself against the door and started banging on it with his fists.

'Harry! Calm down,' Anna protested. Harry threw himself against the door one last time and then sank to his knees, his forehead resting against the cool metal of the door.

'We shouldn't have come in here,' he said as he stood back up.

'Maybe the security men have spotted us,' Nick offered. 'That's why the door has been locked.'

'How can they have spotted us?' Harry protested. 'Where are the CCTV cameras?' He jabbed a finger angrily at the walls of the room.

'So who do you think has locked us in then, Harry?' Anna asked. 'One of the waxworks?' She laughed. 'The one that winked at you?'

'Or the one that squeezed Lucy's hand or the one Nick heard say "Help me"?' Harry snapped. Panic was making him angry – even though he knew this situation wasn't anyone's fault.

Anna looked at Lucy.

'You didn't say anything about that?' she said.

'I probably imagined it,' Lucy said, lowering her gaze.

Anna looked back at Harry accusingly. 'Like I said

before. It's all in the imagination, Harry.' Anna continued walking towards the silver throne in the middle of the room. 'I mean, nothing's happened to me, has it?' She sat down on the throne and smiled at Harry.

He saw the defiance in her gaze as she reached for a small bunch of grapes from a nearby silver bowl and ate two.

'Oh, no,' Anna gasped. 'I've eaten some of the food and I'm still alive.'

Nick and Lucy laughed.

'Yeah, come on, Harry,' Nick chuckled, reaching for an apple. 'If we're stuck in here someone will rescue us soon. We might as well enjoy some of this food while we're waiting for them to get us out.'

'Everything will be fine, Harry,' Lucy added, taking some strawberries from a bowl. 'Just chill out.'

Harry turned away and tried the door again. It wouldn't budge.

When he turned back to face his friends, all three of them were seated on the silver throne, eating and laughing.

'Come and join us, Harry,' Anna laughed. 'There's plenty of room.'

Harry hesitated a moment then wandered across to the throne. What was the use? His friends didn't care. And perhaps they were right. Perhaps he was getting spooked over nothing. Lucy and Anna moved apart to allow him some space on the padded seat.

'Pass me that bottle of grape juice, please, Harry,' Nick said, grinning. 'I'm thirsty.'

Harry hesitated. Should they really be tucking in like this?

'Oh, come on,' Nick said. 'It was your idea in the first place to sneak off and meet the rest of the class halfway round the waxworks. You said it'd be a good laugh and it has been. Getting something to eat and drink is just a bonus.'

Harry shrugged his shoulders, then handed Nick the bottle of grape juice.

Nick popped the cork and the two girls shouted in delight.

Harry heard movement above them.

A soft swishing noise.

He looked up to see the silver drapes above them falling softly to the mirrored floor. There was a beautiful smell too and Harry realized what it was. As the silver material fell, so did hundreds of pink rose petals. They covered the four friends like soft, fragrant snowflakes.

'That's beautiful,' Anna sighed, cupping some of the petals in her open palm.

Nick raised the bottle of grape juice in salute. Harry smiled at his friend. But something made him look back up at the ceiling.

'Look,' he said quietly.

Everyone gazed up at the ceiling.

'What is that?' Harry asked, pointing.

The other three all craned their necks to see what had been hidden by the silver material.

Harry frowned. 'It's some kind of trapdoor,' he said under his breath, his eyes fixed on the metal partition.

The trapdoor was huge. Almost half the size of the

ceiling. And it was ugly. The thick wrought iron was covered in rust spots and dark stains. It didn't fit with the sleek silver room at all.

Harry heard a deafening scrape of metal against metal. The hatch above them was opening. It slid back, yawning like a huge metal mouth as it opened wider. The grinding screech of metal became almost unbearable.

Harry could feel his heart hammering madly in his chest.

'Now what?' he whispered in fear.

Scalding waves of melted wax poured through the open hatch. Harry had no time to duck or run out of the way. The steaming ooze poured out of the hatch, and the bubbling wax hit him.

Harry turned to help his friends but, blinded and choking, all he could do was listen to their muffled cries of terror as they slowly suffocated under their own layer of scalding wax.

Harry could barely think straight. He thought about the door to the room and tried to force his legs to move in the right direction – to escape. But the wax was already setting. He was trapped.

Frozen for ever.

Frozen in time.

FASHION VICTIM

Becky Masters stepped into the cobbled arcade and smiled. This was shopping heaven!

Discreet shopfronts displayed designer goods in their windows. As Becky strolled down the sunlit street, gold-lettered signs swung in the breeze and striped awnings rippled gently.

I could burst with happiness! Becky thought. This is where she belonged. She just wished her parents thought the same. Her allowance wouldn't buy her a carrier bag in these shops.

Glamorous-looking men and women strolled from one boutique to another, expensive bags draped casually over their shoulders. This place was like a private club, hiding from the rest of the town. She was lucky to have stumbled across it last weekend. It would have been so easy to miss the narrow cobbled walkway that led here. Only a discreet sign pointed the way.

As Becky wandered slowly along the arcade, she checked out the outfits in the windows. The shop called Sea You sold swimwear in all colours and styles. Becky loved the electric-blue swimsuit with the panel cut from the middle. She could just see herself wearing that on the beach. Next door was a shoe shop: Save Our Soles. Becky stopped by the shopfront and peered through the plate glass of the window. Beautifully stitched cowboy boots sat next to high-heeled sandals and kitten-heel slingbacks.

And not a price tag in sight, she thought. Becky remembered what her dad had once told her: 'If you have to ask the price then you can't afford it.'

But it was the shop in the centre of the arcade that drew Becky like iron filings to a magnet. She walked over to it, trying not to break out into a run. She already knew what kind of clothes it sold – the best kind.

She stood in front of the window, gazing at the display. It was her idea of heaven. Appliquéd denim jeans, silk scarves, sequinned shrugs and T-shirts with countless different designs and logos on them. They were all displayed on mannequins in catwalk poses, their hips jutting out jauntily. Becky could see that every item was superbly tailored. But there was a new creation in the window that took Becky's breath away. A magnificent red dress. The fish-tail hem casually skimmed the floor of the window display, the folds of satin glimmering in the sunshine. But it was the dress's bodice that Becky found mesmerizing.

It had an inbuilt corset, intricately embroidered with silk and decorated with tiny gleaming crystals that sparkled. The mannequin stood at an angle so that people in the street could see the superb craftsmanship at the back of the dress. The corset was fastened at the back with long crimson laces that pulled the bodice tight. Even the laces had crystals sewn into them. It was a stunning piece of work.

Becky studied her own reflection in the shop window, trying to imagine what she would look like in the dress.

'To die for!' she whispered under her breath.

If only she was able to wear something like that in the charity fashion show this coming weekend. Becky enjoyed her occasional appearances as a model but she had never had a chance to wear anything as stunning as that red dress. If only . . .

Then she had an idea. Becky nodded to herself and strode towards the shop's doorway.

The bell above the door of the clothes shop tinkled as Becky walked in. She glanced quickly at the magnificent red dress as she walked past the window display. The silk was so radiant it almost glowed.

Becky dragged her eyes away from the dress.

The shop had a polished hardwood floor that matched the three counter tops. In the centre of the shop there was a wood and glass table. A blouse, a pair of narrow-legged trousers and some custom-made jewellery were carefully laid across it.

Becky wandered slowly around the small shop, gazing along the racks of clothes and reaching out a hand to gently stroke the folds of fabric. But her attention kept returning to the red dress – she couldn't resist it.

Becky walked across to the window display again. She did some quick calculations in her head. The dress might be a little long for her. But with a pair of high heels? *It would look fabulous*, she thought.

She reluctantly turned away from the dress and walked back across the shop. There were two doors behind the counter. Becky knew from her previous visits that one of them led to the changing room and that the other hid the staff room.

When no one came to attend to her, Becky leaned across the counter to ring the brass bell. But something she saw on a shelf behind the counter made her pause. Becky smiled. They were dolls.

Each one was carved from wood, their faces and hands meticulously painted. Their large, lidless eyes fixed Becky with blind stares. There was something strangely familiar about the dolls. Becky looked back to the racks of clothes . . . That was it! Each doll wore an exact miniature replica of an outfit that was for sale in the shop. One of the dolls was dressed in a small copy of the blouse that lay on the table in the centre of the shop. Another was wearing a deep-blue V-neck sweater decorated with sequins. But it was the doll stood a little apart from the others that Becky was most mesmerized by.

It wore an exact copy of the red dress in the window. The tiny ribbons on the miniature corset were even decorated with minute crystals. It was a perfect replica.

Becky leaned closer and reached out her hand to touch the corset.

'Can I help you?'

Becky spun round at the sound of the voice.

It was Sadie, the owner of the shop and the designer of the clothes.

She was a tall, elegant-looking woman with gorgeously thick, dark hair that reached to the middle of her back. She was dressed from head to foot in green. Even the boots she wore matched her jumper and trousers. On her fingers were large silver rings and as she placed her hands on the counter, Becky couldn't help a stab of jealousy as she noticed the woman's perfect French manicure. What Becky wouldn't do for a manicure like that!

'Hi, Sadie,' Becky began. 'I've been in before.'

'Yes,' Sadie said. 'You've never actually bought anything though, have you?' Sadie stepped neatly behind the counter and smiled at Becky. But Becky could see that the smile didn't go anywhere near Sadie's eyes.

'Your prices are a bit beyond me,' Becky said, trying to smile back. Sadie turned her back on Becky and smoothed a hand over the piles of cashmere jumpers that filled the shelves behind the counter.

'Few people can,' Sadie said over her shoulder. 'But then again, one gets what one pays for. My creations are unique.'

Becky nodded dumbly, trying not to feel embarrassed. An icy silence descended as Becky struggled to find something to say. But she'd come in here with a plan – she had to see it through!

'I was looking at the dress in the window,' Becky said. 'It's really cool.'

Sadie turned round and raised an eyebrow. She walked over to the window display and Becky followed her. Another customer walked into the shop and Sadie nodded a discreet greeting to the woman. For the first time that day, Becky realized how old and tired her outfit looked. She folded her arms across her chest protectively.

'Cool?' Sadie asked. 'It's been called elegant, sophisticated and charming – but cool is not a word that has ever been used in connection with any of my creations. I assume I should take that as a compliment?'

What is your problem? Becky thought. But she couldn't

afford to take offence now. She was still working her way up to asking the all-important question.

'I love the dolls too,' she said, desperate to keep the conversation going.

'Yes, I make miniature versions of each outfit I'm commissioned to create,' Sadie explained. Becky walked towards the counter where the dolls sat, Sadie following closely. 'It's all part of the creative process. I trial the outfits in miniature before I go to the expense of working up a full-size version.'

'This one is brilliant,' Becky smiled, and she reached out to touch the doll dressed in the miniature red dress.

'Don't touch that,' Sadie snapped, whisking the doll out of Becky's reach. Becky stepped back from the counter, surprised by the strength of Sadie's reaction.

Becky watched as Sadie locked the doll away in a cupboard behind the counter.

'Sorry,' Becky said. 'I wouldn't have damaged it. I just wanted to look.'

'I don't like people handling the dolls,' Sadie rasped.

'Now, I assume you did come in here for a reason?'

'Yes, it was about that red dress in the window,' Becky told her. It was now or never. 'I was wondering if I could try it on.'

Sadie laughed scornfully.

'The clothes in this shop are haute couture. Do you understand what that means?'

'I'm not sure,' Becky admitted.

'Well, for one thing it means that they're distinctive,' Sadie told her. 'That dress will remain in the shop window for a week. Then it will be collected by the person who's bought it. I don't think Miss Barton would be too happy if she knew that any Tom, Dick or Harry was walking in here and trying on her clothes, do you?'

'Miss Barton?' Becky said. 'Daisy Barton? About my height and build? Blonde hair? Lives in that really big house?'

Sadie looked shocked, then she nodded slowly.

'I know Daisy,' Becky announced. 'We're friends. We go to the same school. We've modelled together at shows before. I'm sure she wouldn't mind if I tried the dress on.'

'Impossible,' Sadie insisted.

'I can ring her on my mobile and ask her if she minds,' Becky said.

'I wouldn't waste your time,' Sadie said.

'It's no bother,' Becky insisted, pulling her mobile out of her bag.

'No,' Sadie said. 'There's no chance of you trying the dress on.'

'I know I can't afford anything in here,' Becky said. 'But that doesn't mean I can't try things on.'

'Oh yes, it does,' said Sadie, turning to wrap up the silk scarf that the other woman had taken to the counter. Becky was desperate now.

'I've been modelling for nearly ten months now!' Becky burst out. 'And I am again on Saturday. I have connections! I could mention your name to the other models. I'm sure they'd love to spend some of their hard-earned cash in your boutique.'

Sadie raised a curious eyebrow.

'Modelling what?' she asked.

'Clothes, of course,' Becky said. 'In the charity fashion show.'

'Well, you'll see the red dress up close then, won't you?' Sadie sneered. 'Because Miss Barton is wearing it for that same show.'

Becky felt her spirits sink. No matter what she wore on the catwalk, it could never match the red dress that Daisy would be wearing. The shop bell rang out brightly as the one other customer left the shop.

'Now, if you don't intend to buy anything, I'd like to get back to work,' Sadie said. 'I have another outfit I'm designing for someone who is actually going to pay for it.'

Becky turned away from the counter and headed for the door, allowing herself one last lingering look at the red dress as she made her way out. Becky had been stupid to think she'd ever be allowed to try it on. Good job she already had another plan . . .

* * *

As Becky made her way along the arcade and back towards the bus stop, she pulled out her mobile phone. She found Daisy's home number and rang it.

She walked out of the arcade as she waited for it to be answered.

'Hello,' Daisy said.

'Daisy, it's me, Becky.'

'Hey, Becks, where are you?' Daisy asked. Daisy and Becky weren't best friends, but they sometimes hung round together after school and at weekends. Becky liked Daisy – though she knew she could never hope to be in the same league as her. Daisy was beautiful and popular – and her family was loaded. Becky thought she was lucky Daisy even bothered to speak to her.

'I've just been wandering around town,' Becky explained. 'I saw that red dress you're wearing for the fashion show at the weekend. It's absolutely beautiful. You're so lucky.'

'You should have asked Sadie if you could try it on,' Daisy said.

'I did,' Becky explained. 'She wasn't very keen, to put it mildly.'

Up ahead, she could see her bus pulling in to the stop.

'Listen, Daisy, my bus has just arrived,' Becky said, breaking into a run. 'I'll call you when I get home, right?'

'OK, Becks,' Daisy said. 'Talk to you later.'

Becky ran for the bus and caught it just in time. She wandered to the back and slumped into a seat, gazing out of the window. She would definitely ring Daisy again when she got home. There was something important she had to talk to her about.

'I didn't even know you were wearing that dress until Sadie told me,' Becky said down the phone. 'When I saw the dress in the window of her shop I couldn't get over how amazing it looked and then, when I found out it was yours . . .' Becky allowed the sentence to trail off.

She sat on her bed, the cordless phone pressed to

her ear. Her own outfit for the fashion show was hanging on her wardrobe door. It was a white, long-sleeved T-shirt with a black leather, fur-trimmed gilet waistcoat and a pair of three-quarter-length black denim jeans, the outside seams of which were reinforced with strips of studded leather.

Very funky, Becky thought. *But not in the same league as Daisy's dress.*

'Listen, Daisy,' Becky said. 'We should get together pretty soon and try on our outfits together. Then we can decide how we're going to do our hair and make-up for the show.'

And I can try on that red dress, Becky thought, smiling.

'Good idea, Becks,' agreed Daisy. 'But I'll need to pick up my dress from the boutique first.'

'How about tomorrow?' Becky suggested. *Then I'll be able to enjoy the look on Sadie's face when I walk in with you.*

'Cool,' said Daisy. 'We can get the bus into town after school, pick up my dress, then go back to your house.'

Becky smiled as she put the phone down. Her plan

was coming together perfectly. She stood up and walked across her bedroom towards the full-length mirror. Becky studied her reflection in the glass and smiled.

'So, Sadie,' she said aloud. 'I can't try the dress on? We'll see.'

'Who are you talking to?'

Becky spun round to see her little sister peering around the door, one of her favourite dolls clutched in her hand.

'I thought I told you to knock,' Becky said as Ruth walked into the room.

'Who were you talking to?' Ruth repeated.

'Nunya,' Becky smiled.

'Nunya?' Ruth repeated, looking puzzled.

'Yes,' Becky continued. 'Nunya business.' She laughed. 'Now clear off. Shouldn't you be setting the table or doing whatever it is that ten-year-olds do when they're not annoying their sisters?'

Ruth stuck her tongue out and ran out into the corridor.

Becky listened to her sister's retreating footsteps. Then she turned back to the mirror. Tomorrow, she would be wearing the red dress. She couldn't wait.

'I've been thinking about this all day,' said Becky as she and Daisy walked along the little arcade of shops. Daisy nodded and the two girls paused to look at a pair of shoes in the window of a shop.

'I like those,' Daisy said, pointing at a pair of silver high-heeled strappy sandals.

'Me too,' Becky agreed. 'If you get them, I can borrow them. After all, we take the same size in shoes.'

Daisy laughed and stroked a hand through her shoulder-length blonde hair. What Becky wouldn't do for long, blonde hair! She pulled a hand roughly through her own tangled curls.

'Come on, let's pick up my dress. I'm looking forward to trying it on,' Daisy said, linking an arm through Becky's.

So am I, Becky thought, smiling.

As they approached Sadie's shop, Becky slowed her

pace to gaze at the stunning red dress in the window. Daisy pushed open the door. The bell above the entrance tinkled. Becky followed her friend inside.

Sadie got up from behind the counter and looked at the two girls.

She smiled at Daisy but Becky watched the smile fade as Sadie spotted her. Becky tried hard not to feel hurt.

'Hi, Sadie,' Daisy said, noticing the look on Sadie's face. 'This is my friend, Becky.'

'Hello, Daisy,' Sadie murmured, and nodded stiffly at Becky. 'Yes, I've met your friend before.'

As she spoke, Sadie's hand moved protectively towards the doll that wore the replica of Daisy's dress.

'I'd like to take my dress home and try it on, please,' Daisy said.

'Well, if you must,' Sadie stammered. 'It's just that it's been attracting rather a lot of attention. A number of people have commented on it since it's been in the window.'

'We need to try our outfits on so we can plan our

hair and make-up ready for the fashion show,' Becky cut in, smiling.

Sadie's face remained impassive.

'I understand that,' she said flatly. 'But, as I said, the dress has attracted a lot of attention. I was hoping to be able to display it for a little while longer.'

'Well, can't you just display the replica of the dress that's on the doll?' Becky offered, nodding in the direction of the little figure. 'After all, you said that you make exact copies of the full-size creation. People will still be able to see how brilliant the dress is but just in miniature.'

Sadie sucked in a deep breath.

'Yes, but the doll isn't going to be seen by people passing by in the street, is it?' she said.

'You could always put the doll in the window,' Becky suggested cheekily.

Daisy chuckled.

Sadie shot a furious look at Becky.

'So, if I could take the dress now, please, Sadie,' Daisy asked.

Sadie nodded and strode towards the window where she began to remove the dress from the mannequin it was on.

'You'll have to get your mother to tighten the corset, Daisy,' Sadie said. 'She'll make sure it's done properly.'

'I'll help,' Becky told her. 'After all, we're going to be trying the clothes on together anyway.'

Sadie looked sharply at Becky.

If looks could kill! Becky thought, delighted with herself.

'I was wondering what I'd look like in the dress,' Becky said, continuing to tease Sadie.

'I told you yesterday,' Sadie snapped, pulling the dress free. 'This creation was hand-made to Daisy's individual measurements. It was made for her and her alone.'

'We're practically the same size,' Becky told the shop owner.

Sadie returned to the counter with the dress and began wrapping it in tissue paper.

'Could I take the doll too?' Daisy asked, eyeing the model and its miniature dress. 'I know what you said before but—'

'No,' Sadie snapped. 'No. The doll must remain in the shop.'

'But if Daisy's having the dress, why can't she have the doll too?' Becky wanted to know.

'I don't want the doll to leave the shop,' Sadie hissed. Becky was going to say something else, but the look on Sadie's face made her stop. Becky looked at Daisy to see if she could see it too, but Daisy was busy picking the dress up and carefully putting it in her bag.

'Ready?' Daisy asked.

'As I'll ever be,' Becky said brightly.

Daisy and Becky turned towards the shop door. Becky pulled open the door and waited for Daisy.

'Hold on a minute!' Sadie called out. Becky watched Sadie whisper something into Daisy's ear. Becky couldn't hear what Sadie said but Daisy looked over at Becky and laughed. Daisy strolled over to Becky.

With a nod of her head, Daisy indicated that it was time to leave. She walked out of the shop door, swinging her bag carelessly.

Becky took one last look at Sadie, then ran out into the cobbled street to catch up with Daisy.

Becky stood in front of the full-length mirror in her bedroom and inspected her reflection.

'What do you think?' she said, turning to look at Daisy who was sat on the bed, applying eyeshadow. Daisy looked up and Becky pointed at her and began to laugh.

'What?' Daisy asked, grinning.

Becky gestured at Daisy's eyes.

'You've got green eyeshadow on one eye and blue on the other,' Becky told her.

'Oh, I can't make up my mind which looks best,' Daisy said. Then she scanned Becky from head to toe and nodded firmly.

'I know this outfit isn't as good as your dress but it's OK, isn't it?' Becky asked.

'You look great, Becks,' Daisy said. 'I like that shade of make-up on your eyes too.'

'What about my hair?' Becky asked. 'Up?' She grabbed a handful of her long brown hair and scrunched it up on the top of her head. 'Or down?' She let go of the hair.

'Up,' Daisy said.

'It's about time you tried on your dress,' Becky said, nodding towards the beautiful red creation hanging on the door of her wardrobe. 'I can't wait to see what it looks like on.'

Daisy wiped the eyeshadow from her eyelids with a tissue and got up off the bed.

'I'll take it into the bathroom,' she said, carefully pulling the dress off the hanger.

Becky leaned close to the mirror on her dressing-table to apply some lip-gloss. She hoped Daisy wouldn't notice her dad's collection of cheap aftershave in the bathroom.

'What do you think?' Daisy asked as she walked back into the bedroom. Becky turned round from the mirror. It was amazing. The dress was everything she thought it would be.

'Oh, wow, Daisy,' Becky said enviously, gazing at her friend. 'You look stunning.'

Daisy blushed and looked down at herself. 'Do you think so?' she asked shyly.

'That dress is so cool,' Becky said, walking over to her friend to look more closely at the outfit. 'And with you having blonde hair too, it really makes the red material look more intense.'

Becky watched as Daisy walked over to the full-length mirror and looked at herself.

'Can you fasten the laces at the back of the corset part for me, please, Becks?' Daisy asked.

Becky caught hold of the laces in the corset and pulled them tight. Both of the girls laughed as Daisy had to lean away from Becky to hold still. It was amazing to see how the corset exaggerated Daisy's silhouette.

'I suppose Sadie had to do this for you when you first tried it on,' Becky offered, pulling tighter on the laces.

'Her assistant did,' Daisy said, smiling hesitantly. She caught Becky's glance in the mirror, then gazed down at her feet.

'What is it?' Becky asked.

'Well, it's the weirdest thing,' Daisy said. 'But you know the little doll Sadie had with the replica of this dress on? I could swear I spotted Sadie pulling the corsets tight on the doll, back in her office. And it's probably my imagination . . . but it felt as though I could feel *my* corset getting tighter!'

The two girls laughed.

'I think that's called an overactive imagination,' Becky said. She finished tying the strings of the upper part of the dress and stepped back. Daisy turned to face her.

'That is a dress to die for,' Becky said, sighing. She couldn't wait to ask to try it on. But as she started to form the question in her head, Ruth burst into the room. Becky couldn't believe it! There was her sister, as per usual, ruining things.

'I've told you to knock before you come in, Ruth,'

Becky said as her younger sister wandered into the room, carrying one of her dolls in her hand. 'What do you want?'

'I heard you laughing,' Ruth said. She gazed round the room at the make-up and hairbrushes lying around. 'Can I join in?'

'No!' Becky told her. Then she smiled again as she saw her sister look at Daisy. Ruth's mouth fell open and she dropped her doll to the floor.

'You look beautiful, Daisy,' Ruth said, in awe. 'You look like a film star. Is that the dress you're wearing for the fashion show?'

'No, it's her new school uniform,' Becky said, trying to usher her sister out of the bedroom.

'But she looks like a princess,' Ruth said.

'Thanks, Ruth,' Daisy said, blushing again.

'Yes, thanks for your opinion, Ruth,' Becky echoed. 'Now push off and leave us and our make-up in peace.'

'She's all right, Becks,' Daisy said. 'She can stay if she wants to.'

'No, she can't,' Becky insisted. 'She'll end up

borrowing our lipsticks. She's always doing that.' Becky looked at her sister. 'Aren't you? We should call you "Light-fingered Ruth".'

'You're making me sound like a thief,' Ruth protested.

Becky held the door open and stood beside it. 'Bye, Ruth.'

Ruth hesitated, then she picked up her doll and reluctantly walked out of the bedroom. Becky closed the door behind her.

'I'd better be going,' Daisy said. 'I didn't realize what the time was.' Becky panicked. Not yet! Not before she'd had a chance to try the dress on!

'Daisy,' Becky said quietly. 'Look, I feel a bit embarrassed asking but . . . Well, could I try your dress on? Just to see what it looks like? I've thought how beautiful it was since the first time I saw it in Sadie's shop.'

'Of course you can,' Daisy smiled.

'You won't tell Sadie I tried it on, will you?' Becky asked.

'What's it got to do with Sadie?' Daisy asked. 'It's my dress. If I say you can try it on, then you can try it on.'

Daisy reached her arms behind her back and started loosening the laces at the back of the dress.

'I knew you'd ask,' Daisy laughed. 'Sadie said that to me as we were leaving the shop.'

'Is that what she whispered to you?' Becky asked.

Daisy nodded, still unfastening the ties.

'She said you'd ask to try it on,' she answered. 'And that I shouldn't let you. Well, tough. I say you can. Why does she have to be such a witch about it?'

Daisy went to the bathroom and a few minutes later reappeared in her own clothes. She walked over to Becky and thrust the satin folds of the dress into Becky's hands. Becky let the satin slip over her fingers. She'd never felt anything like it before.

'I'm just going to nip to the loo before I go home,' Daisy said. 'I'll tell you what you look like when I come back,' she called happily over her shoulder.

Becky couldn't believe it. She finally had the dress all to herself. Quickly, she climbed out of her outfit and scrambled into the dress. All the world turned a deep red as she pulled the folds of satin over her head and the dress fell down around her body.

It was almost a perfect fit. She stood in front of the mirror and looked at herself. She could hardly believe what she was seeing. This was heaven! But when she reached behind she couldn't reach the laces of the corset. There was no way she could fasten the dress alone. Daisy was still in the bathroom. The only person who could help Becky was her little sister.

'Ruth,' Becky called out. 'Come and help me, please.'

'Ruth,' she called again breathlessly. The waiting was too much! Then Ruth peeped her head around the door of Becky's bedroom, grinning.

'I thought you told me to go away,' Ruth said.

'That was earlier,' Becky said, not taking her eyes from her own reflection. 'I need you to pull the corset tight for me, please.' She turned round to show Ruth the loose laces.

Ruth walked over and reached out for the laces. Then she seemed to hesitate.

'I won't hurt you, will I?' she asked, gazing up at Becky.

'It's all right, Ruth,' Becky assured her. 'Just pull them tight until I tell you to stop.' Ruth took hold of the strings, tugging gently on them.

'If only I had the chance to wear something like this on the catwalk,' Becky said. She sucked in a breath as she felt Ruth pull a little too hard. Becky could feel her ribs resisting the corset.

'Sorry,' Ruth apologized, seeing her sister wince.

'It's fine,' Becky told her, turning from left to right in front of the mirror.

'It really looks good on you, Becky,' Ruth told her.

'Yes, it does,' Daisy added, walking back into the room. 'You look great, Becks.'

Becky smiled broadly and blushed. She suddenly felt self-conscious.

'I'd better give it back to you, Daisy,' Becky said. 'Before I get too attached to it.' Ruth started to pull the laces loose.

'This dress is really amazing,' Ruth said.

'You should take Ruth into Sadie's shop, Becks,' Daisy said. 'Let her have a look at some of the other clothes. Just don't let Sadie know that I let you try the dress on.' Daisy winked.

'That's a good idea,' Becky said happily. 'Would you like to go tomorrow after school, Ruth?'

Ruth's face lit up. Becky could feel herself smiling, too. Taking Ruth to the shop was Becky's perfect opportunity to gloat in front of Sadie. She didn't feel scared of that woman any more. Sadie deserved to know that Becky had tried the dress on. It was about time Sadie realized that even people like Becky — people who didn't have lots of money — could look good in her dresses.

'There it is,' Becky said to Ruth as the two of them walked up to Sadie's shop.

Becky watched as Ruth ran on ahead, her backpack bouncing up and down. Becky's little sister stopped in front of the boutique and pressed her hands against the smooth surface of the window, peering through the glass at the outfits inside. As Becky caught up, Ruth swivelled round on her heel, grinning with delight.

'Come on,' said Becky, pushing the door open. 'Let's go in and have a look around.'

Ruth bounded into the shop behind her and headed straight for a rail of brightly coloured T-shirts. Becky watched as Ruth started at one end of the rail and ran her hand over each garment in turn, eagerly pulling hangers off the rail.

'I hope her hands are clean,' said Sadie, emerging from the rear of the shop.

'She's my sister,' Becky told the designer. 'I told her about your shop and she wanted to see the clothes you made.'

'How charming,' Sadie said dismissively. This was Becky's opportunity.

'Well, she saw the red dress you made for Daisy and she loved it,' Becky said. 'She even thought it looked good on me.'

'You wore that dress?' Sadie asked slowly.

'Chill out, Sadie,' Becky continued. 'Yes, I did. Why shouldn't I?'

Sadie continued to glare at Becky.

'Daisy didn't mind me trying it on,' Becky continued. 'I mean, she'll probably get bored with it in a few months anyway and give it away. Someone will probably end up buying it from a charity shop or something.' Becky smiled.

Becky waited for a reaction from Sadie, but there wasn't one. Becky realized that Sadie wasn't listening to her any more. She was looking at something over Becky's shoulder. She turned to see Ruth leaning over the counter, stretching to touch the wooden doll that still displayed a miniature version of the red dress.

'Leave that alone!' Sadie shouted.

Becky saw that Ruth was pulling the tiny laces at the back of the miniature dress.

'Stop it,' Sadie shouted again, grabbing for the doll.

Ruth backed away, frightened by Sadie's angry reaction.

'I like dolls,' Ruth said. She pointed to three other

dolls lined up behind the counter. 'I've got lots of dolls at home.'

'How interesting,' said Sadie.

'She was just looking, Sadie,' Becky interrupted.

'They're not to be played with,' Sadie said, placing the doll back on the counter. 'They're not toys.'

Ruth looked up at Becky anxiously. Becky jerked her head towards the door and the two of them turned to leave. But as Becky walked away, Sadie followed her.

'I told you not to try that dress on,' Sadie said quietly.

Becky nodded and shrugged. She just wanted to get out of the shop now. 'See you tomorrow at the fashion show. Everyone's going to see the dress then anyway, so I don't know what the big deal is.'

'Come on, Becky,' Ruth called, dashing out of the shop into the arcade. 'Let's go home.'

'Good idea, Ruth,' Becky said. 'I don't think we're very welcome here.'

Sadie held the door open for Becky who smiled politely and stepped outside.

'See you tomorrow,' Becky said just before the door closed behind her. She hurried after Ruth. Her moment of victory with Sadie had left Becky with a hollow feeling in her stomach. It hadn't felt very good at all. And there was something about Sadie . . . *Why* was she so concerned about someone else trying on Daisy's dress? Never mind. Becky would have a great time at the catwalk show tomorrow and she could put all thoughts of stupid Sadie behind her.

'Now, you're going to be all right here, aren't you, Ruth?' Becky asked, raising her voice to make herself heard above the noise of the crowd.

Ruth squirmed in her seat, hugging her back-pack close to her chest. Becky took the backpack out of Ruth's hands and stored it safely beneath Ruth's chair.

'You've got a good view of the catwalk from here,' Becky told her little sister, turning slightly to look at the long platform behind her.

Ruth nodded again but Becky could tell she wasn't

really listening. Ruth was gazing past Becky and up towards the ceiling of the room. Becky twisted round and looked up, too.

It had been covered with swathes of thick black material and large, glittering silver stars and mirror balls hung from the ceiling. It was like a night-time sky, but indoors.

'It's beautiful, Becky,' Ruth sighed.

Becky ruffled Ruth's hair and stood up. The room was already nearly full to bursting with people.

'I've got to get backstage and find out what's going on. Don't forget to clap extra loud when I come on to the catwalk, will you?' Becky said to her sister. Ruth grinned and then ducked her head to look past Becky at the gathering crowds. Becky laughed and turned away.

Becky picked her way through the crowd towards the dressing-room area. Friends and relatives pushed past Becky, eager to get a good seat. She could feel her nerves building. She'd never thought there would be so many people here! This looked as if it was going to be the biggest audience she'd ever modelled in front of.

Becky slipped through a curtained doorway to the left of the stage. She flinched and put a hand up to her face as harsh spotlights blinded her. Shouts and laughs rang out as the other models dashed past her from room to room. The scent of hairspray hung heavy in the air and mobile phones rang cheerily with good luck messages. It was chaos!

Becky's heartbeat quickened. She loved the adrenalin rush of being backstage.

'Hi, Becky!' someone called out as she ran past in a silk dressing-gown. Becky called hello after the girl, though she had no idea who it was.

'You know where you're going, do you?' another voice said from behind her.

Becky turned to see a tall, thin man dressed in black trousers and a black shirt standing gripping a clipboard.

'You are a model, aren't you?' the man asked.

'Yes,' Becky said.

'Well, I'm the stage manager,' the man told her. 'So can you tell me your name, please? I've got to check it off my list.'

'Becky Masters,' she answered, watching as the man ran his finger down the list of names on his clipboard.

'OK,' he said, ticking her name. 'Number thirteen.' He pulled a sticky-backed tag from the clipboard and stuck it on Becky's hand. 'Your number matches the number on your outfit. They're all hanging up in the dressing area, back that way.' He gestured towards another part of the backstage where there were dressing-tables with mirrors, chairs, tables and rail after rail of clothes.

Beyond the man's shoulder, Becky could see models doing their make-up or hair. Others were practising their catwalk struts. Some were standing around chatting and checking out each other's outfits. Becky could feel her excitement building.

Becky was about to go and find her outfit when she spotted Daisy walking towards her.

'Hey!' Daisy said brightly. 'How are you feeling?'

Becky held out a hand and the two of them laughed as they watched it tremble. Daisy put an arm round Becky's shoulders. 'You'll be fine,' she said.

'Listen, everyone,' the stage manager said, raising his voice. 'I need your attention, please.'

Becky and Daisy turned to face him.

'You've all got your numbers,' the stage manager said. 'You'll be able to find your outfits using those numbers. I'm going to pass out copies of the running order.' He held up a piece of bright-yellow paper. 'And you all need to look carefully at it, OK? It tells you in which order you go on stage.'

A murmur of excitement ran round the room.

'It even tells you the music that you're walking on to,' the stage manager continued, raising his voice again. 'All of you take one of these now, please, then I want you all in your outfits as quickly as possible. Hurry, hurry, hurry.'

Becky and the other models formed a queue and took their copies of the running order from the stage manager. Becky finally got to the front and grabbed a yellow sheet of paper, turning it over impatiently to read the running order. She tried not to notice how damp her palms were as she scanned the list.

'You're on last,' Becky said to Daisy. 'I'm not surprised. Your dress is head and shoulders above anything anyone else is wearing.'

'And you're first,' Daisy said, looking up from the list. 'The opening act!' Becky felt a thrill of pleasure. If she couldn't wear the red dress, this had to be a good second best – opening the show.

'Do you want me to help you with your make-up?' Daisy asked.

'Thanks, Daisy,' Becky said, smiling. 'I just want to check that Ruth's OK first.'

Becky stepped up on to the runway and walked along it until she came to the thick curtains that separated the catwalk from the waiting audience. Daisy followed behind her. As Becky stepped closer to the curtains she could hear the hum of the audience from the other side.

Becky carefully eased one of the curtains back a

fraction and scanned the crowd for her younger sister. Becky could see her next-door neighbour and the boy who lived down the road – and there was Ruth! Sat with her hands beneath her knees, grinning with pleasure.

'Can you see her?' Daisy whispered in Becky's ear. It was too dangerous for them both to peek out of the curtains – they'd be sure to be spotted. And that would be *so* unprofessional!

'Yes,' Becky said, smiling. 'She's fine. She's down there in the front row. She's been so excited about this fashion show, you'd think she was one of the designers.'

'Speaking of designers,' Daisy said. 'Can you see Sadie?'

'No,' Becky replied, still scanning the crowd. 'There's a reserved seat on the front row opposite Ruth. Perhaps that's where Sadie's going to sit. She must be running late or something.'

'Come on,' Daisy said, turning away. 'Let's go and get ready.'

Becky nodded but hesitated a few moments longer, watching as the seats slowly filled up. This was going to be an awesome show, Becky could feel it in her bones.

She was about to let the curtain drop shut when she felt a hand clamp on her shoulder.

Becky spun round, her heart racing.

She found herself staring into Sadie's face. And it didn't look good.

'Sadie, what's wrong?' Becky asked.

'Where's the doll?' Sadie asked.

'What doll?' Becky enquired.

'The one with the replica of Daisy's dress on it,' Sadie told her. 'The one your sister was looking at when you were in my shop.'

'I don't know,' Becky said. 'Why?'

'Because it's missing,' Sadie said frantically. Sadie's grip was getting tighter and Becky squirmed to get away.

'Well, I haven't seen it,' Becky told her frostily. 'What makes you think I'd know where it is?' Becky looked past Sadie to see where Daisy was, but her friend was long gone.

'The doll went missing after your visit to my shop,' Sadie told her. 'Now, if your sister took it, I need to know.'

'Ruth would never steal anything,' Becky said icily. 'And I don't like you accusing her of it either, Sadie.'

'Please, Becky,' Sadie said, her tone one of distress rather than anger. 'If your sister took that doll you must tell me.'

'Sadie, I'm telling you, Ruth didn't steal your doll,' Becky snapped. Becky turned on her heel and started to march away from Sadie, though she didn't feel anywhere near as sure of herself as she hoped she looked. Becky pushed through a small crowd of models. A shriek of alarm forced Becky to look behind her. Sadie was roughly pushing the models out of her way as she followed Becky. The woman was deranged!

'If she took it I'll forget all about it, but you must get her to give it back,' Sadie begged. 'She doesn't know what she's done. The harm she could do.' Sadie was so desperate that Becky felt compelled to stop and listen.

'To who?' Becky wanted to know. 'To herself? Sadie, you've got to tell me what's going on. What's so important about the doll?'

'It's not just that doll,' Sadie said. 'It's all of my dolls. They're all important. That's why I make them. That's why I must have that one back. Before it's too late.'

'Then tell me what's happening,' Becky demanded. Sadie dragged her hands through her hair. Any designer poise had long gone.

'I'm talking about how dangerous that missing doll is in the wrong hands,' Sadie said. She looked up at Becky desperately. 'But I can't go into details. Now, please, Becky, if your sister has taken that doll then I beg you, get her to give it back.'

'I've already told you, Sadie. Ruth did not steal that doll,' Becky said defiantly. If Sadie couldn't give her a proper explanation, she wasn't going to get involved in this stupid game.

With a huge sense of relief, Becky saw the stage

manager approaching, waving his clipboard back and forth in the air.

'Come on, come on,' he said. 'The show's going to start soon. There isn't time to be standing around chatting. Hurry, hurry, hurry.' He looked at Sadie. 'You are going to have to take your seat out front, I'm afraid. All backstage visitors have to leave now. Thank you.'

Becky watched him turn away to chase after someone else.

'Get the doll back,' Sadie called over her shoulder as she headed out of the wings. 'Before it's too late.'

'Whatever,' Becky murmured under her breath. Ruth wouldn't have taken that doll. Would she?

'Come on, come on,' the stage manager called, ushering Becky towards the dressing area. 'Hurry, hurry, hurry. You're first on to the catwalk, remember. I can't have you holding up the entire show.'

Becky hurried back to change and do her hair and make-up. She had an appointment with a catwalk and she wasn't going to miss it.

* * *

By the time Becky was dressed in her outfit with her hair and make-up done, she had almost forgotten about her latest argument with Sadie.

She was waiting to step through the curtains and on to the catwalk. Her outfit looked pretty good and Daisy had been great at helping with her make-up. Becky couldn't believe how much her friendship with Daisy was growing. Who'd have thought it? Becky being best mates with cool girl Daisy?

'Good luck, Becks,' Daisy said.

Becky nodded. She was too nervous to speak. The beat of a song suddenly filled the room.

'That's your cue,' said the stage manager, putting his hands on Becky's shoulders. 'Get ready.'

The curtains swung open.

'Go!' the stage manager said, almost pushing Becky into the spotlight.

Becky stepped out into the full glare of the lights. A loud round of applause rang out from the watching audience, along with whoops and wolf whistles. What a thrill! Becky didn't hesitate. She strutted confidently out on to the catwalk, glancing left and right.

There was Ruth, watching her in delight and giving her the thumbs-up. And there was Sadie. The designer leaned forward in her seat, glaring across the catwalk at Ruth. Becky felt a prick of outrage, wanting to protect her little sister from that foul woman. But there was nothing she could do. Becky was on the catwalk and for the next few minutes it was her job to strut, pose and smile.

Becky reached the far end of the catwalk and paused to show off her outfit. Then she turned to walk back again. She looked straight at Sadie. She was still staring at Ruth, her eyes narrowed angrily. Becky couldn't believe it! How dare that woman try to intimidate her little sister? A flashbulb popped and Becky stumbled to one side, going over on the heel of her shoe. The audience gasped but Becky managed to right herself before she fell flat on her face. That woman! Sadie had distracted Becky and now she'd almost gone over on the catwalk. But Becky was determined to be professional. She put on her best supermodel smile and headed back up the runway.

The music seemed to grow louder and the room suddenly felt overwhelmingly hot. Becky could feel sweat breaking out on the palms of her hands. But beyond the nerves and the annoyance of Sadie, Becky felt something else. The thrill of attention.

I am loving this, thought Becky. She felt like a supermodel. As she reached the end of the catwalk she did a full turn and winked in the direction of the audience.

She exited behind a curtain to the left of the stage. Girls and boys crowded round her.

'How was it?'

'You looked great!'

'Did you spot anyone in the audience?'

Everyone had a question for Becky.

'That was so cool,' she said. 'It's just a shame that it was over so quickly.'

The next model walked on to the catwalk. Becky wanted to find Daisy and tell her how great it was out there on the catwalk. She'd deal with Sadie later.

She went to the dressing area but there was no sign of Daisy. Two girls were pulling on their outfits and Becky approached them.

'Have you seen Daisy Barton?' she asked. 'She's about my build and height but she's got long blonde hair. She's wearing that dress in the show.' Becky pointed to the red dress wrapped in see-through plastic, hanging on one of the rails.

'I don't know her,' the first girl apologized, almost falling over as she tried to pull on the most incredibly tight pair of leather trousers.

'I know Daisy,' the second replied. 'She went to sit in the dressing-rooms at the back of the building. She said she didn't feel too good.'

Becky nodded and headed out of the dressing area in the direction of the stairs that led down to the changing rooms.

It was cooler down here and Becky felt her skin rising in goose bumps as she made her way down the stone steps. A long corridor stretched away towards the back of the building. Doors led off it on either side.

Becky opened the door of the first room and peered in.

There was a mirror with bare light bulbs around it set on a dressing-table. Clothes were hanging on one of the wall pegs. The room smelled strongly of perfume and hairspray. But there was no one inside.

Becky moved to the next room. And the next. Both were empty. She opened another door and looked in.

Daisy was sitting in a canvas director's chair staring at her own reflection in the mirror.

'Daisy, at last!' Becky said, stepping into the room. Becky gave an involuntary shiver at the coolness. Why wasn't Daisy feeling it? 'I wondered where you were. One of the other girls said you didn't feel well.'

Daisy didn't answer. She just continued staring at her pale reflection, eyes wide. She didn't even seem to notice that anyone had entered the room.

'Daisy,' Becky said softly, approaching her and putting a hand on her friend's shoulder. 'What's wrong?'

Daisy spun round in her seat and grabbed Becky's arm, her fingernails sinking painfully into the flesh.

'Ow, Daisy, that hurts!' Becky protested, trying to pull her arm away.

But Daisy wouldn't let go. She brought her face close to Becky's.

'You've got to take my place,' Daisy hissed.

'Take your place?' Becky stammered. 'I don't understand.'

'On the catwalk,' Daisy blurted. 'I can't go on. I can't do it.'

'Daisy, calm down,' Becky said. 'You'll be fine. It's just a bit of stage fright. I was nervous before I went on but—'

'I can't do it,' Daisy said more forcefully, this time through clenched teeth. 'You'll have to go in my place. You'll have to wear the dress.'

Wear the dress? This was all Becky had ever dreamed of. But now it didn't feel so tempting. No way did she want to see her friend in this state!

'I can't,' Becky protested. 'It was made for you. Besides, Sadie will go mad if she sees me modelling it.'

'I don't care what Sadie thinks,' Daisy gasped.

She stood up out of her chair and grabbed Becky's shoulders. 'I don't care what anybody thinks. I'm not walking out on that catwalk. I can't.'

'Daisy, normally I'd say yes straight away,' Becky said, smiling. 'You know I'd like nothing more than to wear that dress on the catwalk but . . .'

'You've got to do this for me, Becky,' Daisy insisted. 'If you're really my friend you'll do it.'

Becky hesitated.

'Come on,' Daisy said, dragging Becky towards the door with her. 'We'll go and get the dress. I'll help you put it on.'

Becky thought about saying something but realized that it was useless. She walked quickly with Daisy down the corridor to the rail and the red dress.

Daisy roughly pulled the dress off the hanger and thrust it into Becky's arms.

'Put it on,' she said.

'Are you sure about this, Daisy?' Becky asked.

'Is there a problem?' asked the stage manager.

'She's taking my place,' Daisy said, jabbing a finger in Becky's direction.

The stage manager looked at his clipboard.

'I've got you down as wearing it,' he protested. 'Daisy Barton.'

'There's been a change of plan,' Daisy snapped.

'This isn't the way I do things,' the stage manager complained. 'I told all of you that I had a routine I followed. Each girl was to wear the outfit we'd planned.'

'It doesn't matter who wears the dress,' Daisy rasped. 'As long as someone models it, who cares who it is?'

The stage manager shrugged.

'All right,' he sighed. 'There's no time to argue.' He pointed his pen at Becky. 'Just make sure you're ready when I give you your cue.'

Becky nodded. She couldn't believe it. *This is really happening to me!* she thought. *I'm going to wear the dress.*

'Get changed,' Daisy urged, trying to pull the dress over Becky's head. Becky laughed and fought her off.

'Give me a chance!' she said. She walked over to one

of the dressing-rooms, Daisy following close at her heels. The sounds from the fashion show melted away. Becky felt the slippery satin whoosh over her skin as she slipped on the dress. This was more than Becky could ever have hoped for.

'Will you tighten the laces on the corset for me, please, Daisy?' Becky asked.

Daisy took a deep breath and reached out trembling hands to do up the laces. She looked over Becky's shoulder at their reflection in the mirror. Becky could see the colour returning to Daisy's cheeks. She smiled.

'Thanks, Becky,' Daisy said. 'I owe you one.' Becky smiled back – until a sudden pull on the laces made her wince.

'Loosen them a bit, will you, Daisy?' Becky said, feeling the pressure on her ribs and back.

'Sorry!' said Daisy, laughing.

'That's better,' Becky said. Now she could breathe! And the dress did look stunning on her.

'Here are the shoes that go with it,' Daisy said, pushing a pair of high-heeled red sandals at Becky.

She slipped them on and fastened the straps around her ankles.

'How do I look?' she asked.

'You look amazing,' Daisy said quietly. 'Good luck.'

'I'm sorry, Daisy,' Becky murmured, squeezing her friend's hand. 'Sorry you couldn't wear the dress.' Daisy squeezed her hand back.

'Come on,' the stage manager called, ushering Becky towards the curtains. 'Hurry, hurry, hurry.'

'Thanks, Becks,' Daisy called after her. 'Thanks.'

Becky turned to face the curtains, the music swelling in her ears.

'Ready?' the stage manager said.

Becky nodded.

The music built to a crescendo.

The curtains swung open.

Becky stepped out on to the catwalk for the second time. The spotlights seemed even brighter than before. They were dazzling. The music thundered in her ears and, for a second, she felt a little light-headed.

She took a deep breath and stepped on to the

runway. She felt as if she was gliding along.

I'm the headline act! Becky thought. *I can't believe it!* She could hear gasps from the audience as they laid eyes on the red dress for the first time.

Becky slowed her pace slightly, determined to enjoy every second on the catwalk in this magnificent creation.

She looked over at Sadie and tried to smile. But Sadie looked horrified to see Becky in the dress and started to stand up out of her chair. What was she going to do?

Becky would explain why she was wearing the dress after the show. She'd tell Sadie about Daisy's stage fright. Sadie would understand.

Wouldn't she?

But Sadie wasn't looking at the catwalk any more.

Her gaze was fixed on something opposite her.

Becky saw Sadie lunge forward, her lips moving soundlessly.

She was pointing at someone. Becky looked round. The chair that Ruth had been sitting in was empty. But behind the crowd of faces gazing up at the catwalk, Becky could see Ruth. Typical Ruth! She'd got bored and gone to sit beneath one of the refreshment tables at the back of the room. She was probably hoping to be hidden by the velvet tablecloth, but it had ruched up beneath a punch bowl.

She wasn't watching the show. She was playing with something, her backpack open by her side.

'The doll,' Becky whispered under her breath as she saw the small figure her younger sister held.

Becky continued to walk along the catwalk but now her mind was reeling.

Ruth took the doll from Sadie's shop, she thought. How could she? After everything Becky had said to Sadie. Becky looked angrily at her younger sister.

Then the sudden pain in her ribs ripped the breath from her.

Becky stumbled slightly and she heard some of the audience gasp, convinced that she was about to fall.

The pain was still there, getting worse. Becky

clutched her sides. She tried to suck in a breath but could only manage a shallow gasp.

It felt as if someone had clamped her in a huge vice and was slowly tightening the jaws.

Becky's eyes were watering from the pain now and she was finding it difficult to breathe.

What was happening?

She managed to reach the end of the catwalk – just – and turned.

If I can just get off-stage, Becky thought, trying not to panic. She didn't know how much longer she could go without screaming. She felt hot, then cold. She was only half aware of the audience now, figures blurring before her as she noticed people turn to whisper in each other's ears. No one was smiling or clapping any more.

She was sure she was going to faint. The pain was so intense now that she could barely walk. She could feel her mouth opening and closing but, try as she might, she couldn't catch her breath. Her head was spinning and, all the time, the music grew louder in her ears along with the roaring of her own blood.

Again she stumbled and almost fell. Someone cried out in alarm. People were on their feet around the catwalk now, reaching out hands to help her.

Becky's younger sister stayed under the table, oblivious to the action on-stage. Sadie's doll was propped up on her lap. And now Becky saw what Ruth was doing with the doll.

Becky felt another incredible surge of pain around her chest and stomach. What little air was left in her lungs was being forced out.

Ruth pulled even more tightly on the doll's corset, her face set in lines of concentration.

Becky felt herself blacking out. She knew she was losing her balance. She was level with Ruth when she finally lost her footing. Becky hit the catwalk hard and lay looking at her younger sister.

Someone in the audience screamed.

Becky could taste blood in her mouth. The pain around her chest was unbearable now. She felt as if a massive invisible fist was crushing her.

And still Ruth pulled harder on the doll's strings, tightening the miniature red dress.

Becky felt herself losing consciousness and she tried to call out to Ruth that she had to stop. She opened her mouth but all that came out was a throaty gasp.

Ruth pulled fiercely on the strings.

Becky winced in agony and felt two of her ribs snap like twigs.

She couldn't breathe.

There was no more air in her lungs. White stars danced before her eyes.

The last thing she saw was Sadie lunging towards Ruth.

In those last seconds, Becky finally understood what Sadie had been warning her about. She wished she'd never walked past that shop window, never seen the dress, never taken Ruth to the boutique. But it was too late now.

She felt one more savage explosion of pain.

And then there was nothing.

Terrify yourself with more books from Nick Shadow's
Midnight Library

Vol. I: *Voices*
Kate knows that something is wrong when she starts hearing voices in her head. But she doesn't know what the voices mean, or what terror they will lead her to . . .

Vol. II: *Blood and Sand*
John and Sarah are on the most boring seaside holiday of their lives. And when they come up against the sinister Sandman, they really begin to wish they'd stayed at home . . .

Vol. III: *End Game*
Simon is a computer addict. When he's sent a mysterious new game, the lines between virtual reality and real life become terrifyingly blurred . . .

Terrify yourself with more books from Nick Shadow's
Midnight Library

Vol. IV: *The Cat Lady*

Chloe never quite believed her friend's stories about the Cad Lady. But when a dare goes horribly wrong, she finds out that the truth is more terrifying than anyone had ever imagined . . .

Vol. V: *Liar*

Lauren is shy. She just wants a friend, and she's so lonely she even imagined herself one. But she soon realizes she'd created a monster. A monster called Jennifer . . .

Vol. VI: *Shut your Mouth*

Louise and her mates love to get their sweets from Mr Webster's old-fashioned shop, but when their plan to get some of the new 'Special Delights' goes wrong, could they have bitten off more than they can chew?

Terrify yourself with more books from Nick Shadow's
Midnight Library

Vol. VII: *I Can See You*
Michael didn't want to move out of the city in the first place. And wandering round the countryside in the dark really isn't his idea of fun – particularly when he finds out how dangerous the dark can be . . .

Vol. VIII: *The Catch*
David and Adam aren't too worried when they get lost on the open sea. But when they discover an abandoned boat in the fog, things start to turn nasty. Who – or *what* – lies in wait beyond the waves . . . ?

Vol. IX: *The Whisperer*
Rachael has always wanted to be a journalist, so writing for the student paper is a perfect opportunity. But then her column begins to write itself, and soon no subject is safe . . .